Realms of Fantasy

Realms of Fantasy

Mychael Black
and Shayne Carmichael

A SAMHAIN PUBLISHING, LTD. publication.

Samhain Publishing, Ltd.
577 Mulberry Street, Suite 1520
Macon, GA 31201
www.samhainpublishing.com

Realms of Fantasy
Copyright © 2009 by Mychael Black and Shayne Carmichael
Print ISBN: 978-1-60504-113-1
Digital ISBN: 1-59998-905-0

Editing by Linda Ingmanson
Cover by Anne Cain

First Samhain Publishing, Ltd. electronic publication: April 2008
First Samhain Publishing, Ltd. print publication: February 2009

HUNTER AND THE PREY

Chapter One

"Is that him?"

Lev nodded, giving only a noncommittal sound in response. He had been tracking this one for nearly four years, and every time he came close to striking, the foul creature would flash a dark smile his way then disappear without a trace. This time, Lev was determined to succeed. This game of cat-and-mouse was getting old.

"Is it time?" the younger one beside him asked, almost under his breath. Lev couldn't blame him, really. He'd been nervous on his first mission, too.

"Not yet." Just a bit longer, Lev neglected to add.

Despite his annoyance with this game, Lev found himself seeking this demon out...for his own purposes. Ebony hair that shimmered blue in the moonlight drew a straight line for Lev's eyes to follow, down the exquisite form of a male body. Dark eyes laughed at him, mirroring the devilish smile, every time they crossed paths. This time was no different, but once again Lev found himself too mesmerized to act when his chance came. Before he could even blink, the creature disappeared in a cloud of blue-black smoke.

"Wow."

The exclamation from the young one beside him told Lev he understood. He stood from where he'd been crouching and stretched his arms over his head. The silver of his wings shimmered in the scant light of a streetlamp, and his gaze lingered where the creature had been.

"Are they all..."

Lev glanced down at the young angel still hunched near his feet. The young one's lack of words conveyed much. "No. They are not all created as the picture of beauty."

The young angel looked back at the empty space, where only moments before the most beautiful creature of Hell had stood. "But he was."

Lev nodded. "Yes. He most certainly was."

Heaven above, what was he thinking? Four years ago, Lev had been sent to hunt this one down, a rogue minion straight from the bowels of Hell, freed by a foolish dabbler in arcane arts and left to wander the Earth. Four years ago, Lev had told many of them they were crazy. They had tried to warn him, tried to tell him of the creature's beauty, but he had not believed them. Until he saw Alael for himself.

Now, he was growing tired of the games. Four years was a long time to harbor a deep-seated ache for something one should never want to begin with.

He waited for the young angel at his side—Simael, his name was. As Simael stood, Lev pushed stray thoughts of

Alael from his mind. This was a training mission, and the last thing he needed was his mind on things other than teaching Simael the fine art of demon-hunting.

"Come." The one word was a clear command, and Lev gave Simael only the slightest glance before lifting into the air.

As they moved unseen above the city, Lev watched the young angel carefully, looking for signs of quick learning. Then Simael dipped, and Lev followed. He sensed the lesser taint and hoped Simael did as well. He smiled as the angel did not disappoint. They landed in the middle of a thickly wooded park. Lev let Simael lead the way, knowing the young one needed to learn to trust his senses. A lesser imp lay in wait in the blackness of an alley, hoping for a hapless soul to wander by, one who would be weak enough to entice. At the sight of the two angels, the imp cowered then jumped, leaping up to the top of the four-story building beside him.

Lev sighed and nodded, waving his hand in the direction the imp had taken. "After you," he said with a wry grin.

For two hours, they chased the imp—a sleek, red-skinned creature with tiny, almost useless wings and razor sharp teeth. No taller than a four-year-old child, the imp was relatively harmless, but he was a menace nonetheless. When they finally cornered him, Lev stood back, letting Simael lead the fight. It was a short one and, with a bolt from Simael's palm and a high-pitched shriek from the imp, the little demon disappeared in sparkles of light. Lev smiled.

"Very good!" He clapped his hand on Simael's back and nodded toward the portal opening before them. "Return now to the Order, and take your rest. We will continue your training next week. I have a good amount to catch up on down here."

"Thank you," Simael said before stepping through the portal.

As the doorway closed behind Simael, Lev sighed. He didn't mind teaching, but his own work went neglected when he did. The Order of Harmony maintained a balance in the physical realms and part of Lev's job was to train the younger angels.

He turned and started for home, which, for the time being, was nothing more than an oversized loft apartment in a renovated warehouse. On loan from the Diocese of Washington, it was better than most places, especially when one couldn't land a normal job for lack of sufficient—and believable—identification.

As he neared the warehouse, Lev's mind wandered back to the one place he knew it should not venture. Yet no matter how hard he tried, he always thought of Alael, the sinfully graceful devil who had captured his imagination...in more ways than one. If the Higher-Ups knew what was going on in his head, Lev would never hear the end of it. While it wasn't an issue that was entirely forbidden, it was certainly frowned upon. Lev knew the rumors would run rampant if word got out that he fantasized regularly about a demon.

He had just started down the sidewalk that led to the

main entry of the building when he felt an all-too-familiar presence. He stopped walking and closed his eyes, all the while trying desperately to reign in his insanely beating heart. This time was different. He could feel it. He was now the hunted.

Turning in a slow circle, he looked around the deserted parking lot. Aside from the few cars belonging to church officials, he saw nothing. Yet the feeling of being watched remained, and Lev knew he had a choice. Alael was giving him a choice: destroy him, or give in. And that was the question that loomed in Lev's mind, as his head told him to destroy the demon once and for all, but his heart? Now that was a whole different story.

"Funny how the hunter can easily become the hunted."

Lev spun around, knowing that voice well. Its rich tone had haunted him for four years, speaking to him in the dead of night, when his fantasies drove him to the brink of madness. Now he stood, once more face to face with the very demon he had vowed to destroy, and yet he couldn't bring himself to move a single muscle.

Alael stepped out of the darkness near a corner of the building, his black feathery wings settled against his back as he approached Lev. Stalked was a better word, really, as the demon's movements were sleek and graceful like a cat's. Lev knew, if he were to give into his darkest fantasies, the demon would purr...and growl. Both sounds echoed in Lev's mind every time he climaxed at his own hand.

"I could destroy you easily," Lev said, exuding a calm he certainly did not feel.

"Ah," the demon said with a soft, silky purr. "But you won't." He stopped close to Lev; too close. When he reached out, Lev stepped back. Alael's forked tongue slid across his lips as the dark depths of his eyes reflected what Lev had always fought to control.

"And what makes you think that?" Lev continued to back away, unaware of how much room he had left to move. Before he was ready for it, he backed right up against the cold brick wall of the warehouse.

Alael closed in on him until their bodies were an inch apart. Lev's breath caught in his throat as Alael smiled. With a speed that left him dizzy, Lev found himself pinned tightly to the wall, with a demon's tongue darting down his throat. A momentary lapse of reason and he tangled his fingers in Alael's hair, holding it in a painful grip as he deepened their kiss. Every inch of him, from the inside out, flamed with an unholy fire, and only when Alael's hands left the wall to slide across his wings, did Lev come to his senses. He shoved the demon away and took off, darting around the corner.

Alael's laughter followed him all the way up to his third-floor apartment, and Lev slammed the door shut, falling against it in a breathless heap. After several minutes of trying to collect his wits, he pushed away from the door.

A shower; that's what he needed. Perhaps it would wash away the lingering scent of Alael, that sharp, soul-consuming smell of earth and fire and lust. As he walked to the bedroom, Lev stripped out of his clothes, tossing his pants and shirt into the laundry basket in front of the washing machine as he walked by it.

Once in the bathroom, he started the water, needing it hot and steaming, enough to chase away any thoughts of wanting the fiendish Alael. He stepped into the shower and slid the curtain closed. As the near-scalding water beat down on his body, Lev was finally able to breathe normally again. For the first time since Alael cornered him, he started to think clearly.

It had not been the first advance the demon had made, but it had been the first one Lev gave in to. And how could he not? Alael was built like the angels of Heaven, created in perfect beauty, but for an unholy purpose. Still, he was male. He had the same anatomy as a human male, of which Lev knew more than his share. Loving those of the same gender was not a crime, and it was a pastime that Lev indulged in whenever he could. But to lust after a demon? Now that was something much more.

Lev placed his palms against the shower wall as he hung his head down under the spray. He watched the water swirl down the drain, hoping some of the heat within him would do the same. Heat. Heaven above, Alael had nearly incinerated him. Lev shivered as he remembered the lick of the flames that had surrounded them. With every stroke of Alael's tongue, the flames flared until no part of Lev's body went untouched by the demon's fire.

Lev closed his eyes as his body remembered that blazing touch, the searing kiss he should have never given in to. But, oh, how he had wanted it! Every damning second of it, caught between the demon's body and the cold brick, Lev had wanted more. With a groan, he reached down and ran his fingertips down the length of his cock, now harder than it had ever been. As he stroked himself, he imagined the demon's tongue—that forked length of pure muscle—licking every inch of his body, leaving no bit of flesh untasted.

He rested his head against the wall as his strokes increased. The water, as hot as Alael's touch, pounded his body, bringing to mind images and sensations of Alael's body pounding against his, the demon's cock driving deeper inside him. With a throaty cry, Lev came, releasing his seed into the swirling water. He dropped to his knees then, struggling to bring his breathing under control once more. He couldn't keep on like this. Not if he valued his sanity.

⋘

He'd been watching—and waiting. Alael loved toying with this one. Time had passed, but the demon no longer kept track. He could still taste the sharp, divine sweetness of the angel's breath on his tongue, his fire doing nothing to diminish that pure flavor. And he knew; he knew what Lev did in the privacy of his shower, knew the angel wanted him so much it burned.

Crouching just on the ledge of a building overlooking the bustling street below, Alael waited, tongue sliding across his lips as his gaze followed the angel's movements. To mortals, Lev was a man—albeit one of immense beauty, but to Alael? To Alael, Lev was a drug, one he craved more than the tainted souls he fed on.

Lev kept quiet watch over the surrounding crowd as he moved silently among the humans. For now, nothing disturbed the placid lake of mortal activity, and Lev's duty was to keep it that way. The souls around him went about their business completely unaware of the angel and demon in their midst. Pausing beside an open doorway, Lev looked in before entering the nightclub.

Dropping to the ground, Alael stepped out into the crowd, more focused on the angel's whereabouts than on toying with the mortals around him. Any other time, he would have played with the humans; now he wanted one creature.

As Alael slipped into the bar, he closed his eyes, drinking in the thundering music, the throb of need assaulting him. He could feel the rhythms thrumming through his soul—blood rushing through drugged veins, come splashing, cries of need and completion ringing out. And there, in the midst of it all was the angel he sought.

Lev motioned to the bartender. As he felt an arm slide around his shoulder, he grinned over at his friend Cameron.

"I'm buying the first round then I'll let you buy the

next five." Chuckling, Cameron rested against Lev.

"That doesn't sound like a bargain." Lev dug into his pocket for the money to pay for the drinks as Cameron ordered two whiskeys.

A hand reached across Cameron and plucked demandingly at Lev's shirt. "Girlfriend, get rid of the knit sweater. It's so last year. When are you going to let me dress you?"

"When hell freezes over, Esmie. And I can personally assure you it never will." Lev eyed the gorgeous drag queen and laughed. From the top of her coiffed auburn hair to the tip of her Prada-shod toes, Esmie was an original fashion plate all her own.

A growl started low in Alael's chest as he stared at the arm draped over the angel's shoulder. Lev was his—his! To see someone else touching the angel made the fiery blood in Alael's veins boil. Crossing the room quickly, he made a point to be seen, a shotglass of whiskey appearing before him moments later. The bartender went about his business, the money-wrapped pills passing from Alael to the man's hand in the blink of a mortal eye. As he raised the shotglass to his lips, Alael focused on Lev from across the corner of the bar.

"Move over, bitch." With a nudge of her hip, Esmie pushed Cameron out of the way. "Let me talk to my boy here."

Cameron laughingly gave way and stood on the other side of Lev. Esmie reached back, laying a well manicured hand on Lev's ass. "Damn, babe, something that tight deserves a hell of a lot better than what you're wearing."

With a raised brow, Esmie caught sight of Alael before Lev did. "Oh my, baby boy, don't look now, but somebody else has designs on that fine ass of yours."

Looking up at her words, Lev saw Alael glaring at him. Dragging his gaze away, he muttered, "You two might want to go do something else."

Smirking, Esmie backed off as Cameron looked over at Alael then grinned at Lev. "Make sure he leaves some for me."

Alael stared unblinking at the angel. It took considerable effort on his part to keep from shattering the glass in his hand as another unwelcome hand touched what was his. His dark gaze slid from one unfortunate soul to another then back to focus sharply on Lev's eyes.

After finishing off the last of his whiskey, he all but slammed the shotglass onto the black-lacquered bar and stood abruptly. Without a word, jaw clenched tightly, he walked around the bar and grabbed Lev's arm, tugging him out onto the dance floor with a growl.

Surprise echoed in the angel's expression. Lev tried to resist, but it proved useless, and he glared back at Alael. The demon knew the angel couldn't react as he normally would without causing one massive scene in the club, and Alael knew Lev wanted to avoid that at all costs.

Instead Lev growled out in annoyance, "What is your problem?"

Sliding his arm around the angel's waist in a clearly possessive gesture, Alael jerked Lev hard against his body. "They were touching you," he snarled under his breath, hips beginning to move, grinding against Lev's in time to the steady pulse of the music.

The struggle to not give in to the bruising feel of the demon's body became apparent in Lev's eyes. "Have you lost your wits, Alael?"

Lev fully intended to push the demon away, but he dug his fingers into Alael's arms instead. Echoes of arousal pulsed through Lev with the grinding hardness against him.

Alael tangled his fingers in the angel's hair. Tilting back Lev's head, Alael licked and bit at the hollow of his throat. "You cannot deny this." He breathed the words across Lev's skin and sharp heat flowed over the smooth flesh.

Lev very well could and would. He opened his mouth to refute Alael, but the only sound escaping him became a soft moan as he felt the heat of the demon's tongue against his skin. His fingers tightened on the material of Alael's shirt, and he closed his eyes. The line of his body pressed tighter to Alael. He slid his hands up into the dark hair and tugged Alael down to kiss him hard. He craved the dark taste, and it had started with their first kiss.

Heedless of the other dancers, Alael backed them off the dance floor until he had Lev pinned between him and the wall. As he thrust his tongue deep into Lev's mouth, the demon rocked forward, pressing their bodies together in time to the music surrounding them. Alael sucked and bit at Lev's tongue, snarls and growls filling the angel's mouth as the kiss turned hungry, almost dangerous.

The demon's fire seared Lev with its heat, threatening to consume him as he tasted it again. All rational thought was obliterated.

Esmie's whistle of appreciation disrupted the forbidden concentration and brought Lev back to himself. With a hard push, Lev got Alael off of him and broke for the door to get outside, as far away from the demon as possible.

Knowing the demon wouldn't follow him, Lev leaned against the outside wall of the back parking lot of the club, his breath ragged as he tried to calm the inner turmoil. The ache in his body wasn't easy to ignore, and his pants were damn uncomfortable. Lifting his hands, he rubbed at his eyes.

"Lev?" A hand touched Lev's shoulder, massaging the tense muscles. "What the fuck happened?" Cameron asked.

Lev lowered his hands. Forcing a smile he didn't quite feel, he said with a shrug, "Just somebody I knew from a long time ago."

Cam lifted an eyebrow. "Must have been one hell of a somebody. You needin', baby?" He moved closer, standing in front of Lev as he slid his fingers down the front of Lev's shirt.

All Lev could do was groan. He slid his arms around the young man's waist to draw Cam against him. "When have you known me not to need? It'll wait 'til you're done at the club, though. Just stop by my apartment before you head home, all right?"

"When have you ever known me to turn you down when you're needin'? We took Esmie's car. Let's go." Before he moved, however, Cam leaned in, sliding his tongue into Lev's mouth, kissing him deep and easy.

Lev tried to focus his full attention on Cam, even with the thoughts of Alael intruding. Returning the easy kiss and centering his senses on Cam, he took the kiss to another level. Pulling back, he gave Cam a wry grin. "Keep it up, and we might not make it."

Cam chuckled and tugged Lev out of the alley and toward Lev's apartment. With home only a few minutes away, the walk was quick. Once they were inside the apartment, Cam turned and pushed Lev against the door, picking up the kiss where they'd left off.

"What're you needing, baby?" The kisses moved from Lev's mouth, down his chin, over his neck. Cam's fingers worked Lev's pants open. He wrapped his fingers tight around Lev's cock, giving it a firm squeeze.

A nudge of Lev's hips answered Cam as he shoved his pants the rest of the way down. "Bedroom, Cam. And you on your knees."

Chapter Two

In a brooding mood, Lev made his way behind the old abandoned warehouse. Chasing down a damned imp was tedious work at best, and he'd been on this one's trail for more than fifteen minutes. Slipping through the door that barely hung on its hinges, he entered the building. The smell of decay and waste were stronger here. Not too long ago, humans had been living in this place. Remnants of their usage of the building littered the floor.

"Well, look what we caught ourselves." One of the demons smirked as he stepped forward.

Lev knew he was outnumbered. Several demons swarmed him, their cockiness apparent as they moved closer. Lev's wings outstretched in enraged agitation right before two of the demons tackled him. As they pinned him to the filthy floor, the largest demon—and most certainly the leader of their small coterie—stepped up beside the twisting mass of flesh and feathers.

"Now you are a pretty one," he sneered, licking his lips. "Such purity..." He crouched and slid a finger along the edge of Lev's right wing.

The touch to his wing sent a betraying shiver through Lev. He growled and by sheer force freed one of his hands. He grabbed hold of the demon's throat. The two who held him down had to struggle, and the blond-haired one yelled to his companions for help.

"Get your fucking arses over here and keep him down!"

Scrambling to obey, three others swarmed Lev, each one catching a leg or an arm, pressing him tightly to the floor. Their leader stood and circled the pile of leathery and divine skin, a look of pure amusement on his face.

With inhuman strength, Lev twisted free of his captors before they could get a good grip on him. Jumping to his feet, he regained his hold on the leader's throat and sent the demon crashing into the nearby wall. Three of the others flew at him, dragging Lev back down. Talons clawed into his clothing, tearing it to get to the skin beneath.

Snarling and cursing, the leader pulled himself out of the rubble of broken wood. What had once been the desire to play—albeit roughly—was now the desire to destroy. Gripping one of the lesser demons by the throat, he threw the creature to the side as he stormed his way back toward Lev. Just as he reached the others, he stopped in his tracks.

Blood poured out of his mouth and he looked down, eyes going wide as the hand in front of him tightened into a fist. Seconds later, he dropped to the floor, flesh sizzling as Alael cast the flaming heart aside. The others shrieked, some of them scrambling away into the shadows as Alael started for them.

One of the demons struck at Lev's wing, slashing through the feathers and sinew. Blood welled up from the gashes, staining the pristine silvery white of his wings. The scent of Lev's blood filled the air. Rising to his hands and knees, he tried to shake off the last of the demons. A glowing light flowed over his skin, burning any who touched him. Those left quickly fled. Alael dropped to his knees beside Lev and reached out, growling as the divine light burned his skin while he helped Lev steady himself.

Lev almost struck out before he realized Alael was the one touching him. The fierce flare of light died as he shook his head groggily. Though the demons couldn't have killed him, it would have taken a great deal of his energy to dispatch so many back to where they belonged.

"You aren't safe here." Standing, Alael bent and picked up Lev, brooking no argument as a portal opened before them. Alael stepped through it and into another room—or place. It was nothing more than a one-room apartment, if one could even call it that much. Alael placed Lev on a pallet.

Completely confused, Lev stared. "You're helping me. Why?"

Alael sat back against the wall, pulling up his legs and resting his arms over his knees. "I told you before, and I will keep telling you until you believe it: you are mine."

The idea of an angel in any way belonging to a demon

was far too alien for Lev. "Impossible, Alael."

Directing his attention toward healing the damage, Lev never looked away from the demon. The open wounds began to close, leaving only bloodstains behind. He'd not waste his energy with a little matter like that. Not when he could more easily take a shower later.

"Not impossible." Nodding toward a door across the room, Alael added, "There's a bathroom in there, if you wish to clean up."

"It is impossible." Lev stood abruptly, the twinge of pain in his wing no more than an echoing reminder, a ghost sensation to his senses. He went into the bathroom and stripped out of his clothing. He did waste a small amount of energy mending the ripped fabric. After turning on the faucet in the shower, he stepped under the hot spray. Half hoping to relieve the sudden tension that had sprung up in him, Lev stood beneath the water, eyes closed. He wasn't surprised when he felt Alael step behind him.

"You can't run from the inevitable." Alael's words drifted over Lev's slick skin; his tongue licked away the water along the top of Lev's shoulder. Sliding a hand around Lev's waist, he brought them together, Lev's back to his bare chest. The strength of his hold wasn't easily escapable.

Shock rippled through Lev and desire followed in its wake. The heat of the demon's internal fire drew Lev like nothing else could. "How did you... Why?" Closing his eyes, he fought against the urge to give in, to taste at least once what he'd begun to crave.

"Perhaps you should make a habit of locking the door," Alael whispered gruffly, his tongue snaking out to trace the curve of Lev's ear. One hand slipped between them, tracing a slow line down Lev's spine, just barely skimming the crease of his ass. Alael slid his other hand up Lev's stomach to his chest, grazing one of Lev's nipples with his fingertips.

Lev could force Alael to stop touching him with a simple expenditure of energy, yet he didn't. The betraying shift of his body gave lie to the small noise of protest he made. Pressing back, he wanted far more than the feathering tease of the demon's hand on his ass. He reached for Alael's hip, his nails digging slightly as he covered the demon's hand on his chest with his other.

"Yes," Alael murmured. "You want this. You *need* this."

Moving them forward, Alael bent Lev over, bracing him against the shower wall. Then he stepped back, letting both hands slide slowly down Lev's sides, over his spine, and finally to his ass, fingers spreading Lev open. In one motion, Alael was on his knees and his tongue was pushing into the angel's body, the length of pure muscle sliding deep.

Lev started to argue, but the demon's touch short-circuited his brain. As Alael's tongue entered him, Lev cried out. "Yes, Alael." He clawed at the slick surface of the wall, silently begging for more. The fire spread swiftly through him, igniting an undeniable need. Lev dropped a hand to his cock and stroked it as he moaned.

Alael slipped in two fingers alongside his tongue, stretching Lev open. As he pulled away and stood, he licked a slow path up Lev's spine to the base of his neck. Alael leaned over Lev and plunged his fingers in and out of Lev's body.

The very thing that had crept into his dreams was happening to him, and Lev was powerless to stop it. Heat engulfed him from every touch of the demon's tongue and hands, promising more to come. "Need you, need more. Please, Alael." Each word came with a gasp as he rocked between Alael's hands.

Growling, Alael pulled out his fingers, lined himself up and thrust hard, driving his cock deep inside Lev. Keeping one hand tight on Lev's cock, Alael wrapped the other in the angel's hair, pulling him up and back as he thrust again.

"Yes. Mine." The words were part groan, part growl. Alael's teeth grazed Lev's neck as he slammed into him.

The swift penetration and invasive heat burned through Lev. Shaking his head wildly, he tried to speak, but the words refused to come. Only soft noises rose in his throat, urging the demon to take him completely. He strained toward the demon's touch, the sensations threatening to drag him under.

"Come for me, Lev." His thrusts never relenting, Alael drove them hard, his hand working Lev's cock in time to the movements of his own as it pierced the angel's body. "Come on my cock. I want to hear you scream my name."

Turning Lev's head until he could see the angel's eyes, Alael grazed his thumb over the tip of Lev's cock, pressing into the slit. "Know I'm the one doing this to you." Before Lev had a chance to respond, Alael's tongue pushed into his mouth, tasting and devouring.

Each word echoed in Lev's mind, as relentless as the drive of Alael's hips. As his own pleasure rolled him under, his seed spilled over the demon's hand and a guttural cry forced its way from Lev's throat. Lev drowned under the assault, the demon's name torn from his lips. "Alael!"

Alael roared, ramming hard as he came. Heat poured out of him and deep into Lev. Lev could smell the demon's seed, his sweat. In the aftermath, he closed his eyes, letting his mind follow the heat of Alael's essence. As the waves pervaded him at the deepest levels, he limply fell back against Alael. Barely able to support himself, he shook his head as if to stop the flood. His thoughts scrambled to catch up, to ask what Alael was doing to him, but he couldn't talk. All he could do was drown beneath the flames scorching his very soul.

"Mine." The word drifted from Alael's mind to Lev's, burning the truth of it into both of their souls, sealing them.

Alael reached out. His hand caught the metal bar on the shower wall and he sank to his knees, slipping out of Lev and pulling the angel down with him.

Lev remained limp as he leaned heavily against the demon. There were no barriers or shields in place to stop

Alael's claim on him. Twisting in Alael's arms, Lev burrowed against him.

"Shh," Alael murmured, kissing Lev's hair softly. "Come. Bed."

He turned off the water and stood, lifting Lev. He carried him to the pallet then went back for towels, kneeling to dry Lev off before drying himself. He had no idea what had happened, and just now he wasn't inclined to ask. Instead, he pulled the angel close as he slid under the blankets.

у

How could he have so far forgotten himself? The question ran through Lev's thoughts incessantly. Keeping Simael on a vigorous training routine hadn't kept Lev's mind from lingering over everything that had happened between him and Alael. He knew the moment the demon tried to call him, and he completely resisted it. No way would he answer, even as the urge grew stronger throughout the course of the day.

Instead, he and Simael continued hunting through the city, scouring every dark corner. If some of Lev's attacks seemed more than a little vehement, Simael kept his mouth shut. Cornering a small pack led by only one demon, Simael handled the smaller creatures while Lev dealt with the larger.

Simael skillfully kept the imps contained to the small portion of the alley they were in. His ability had increased considerably since Lev had taken on his training. Leaving the young angel to handle it, Lev quickly followed the demon trying to escape into the air. With a minute expenditure of power, Lev had hold of the demon before it could even clear the buildings.

Snarling at Lev, he screeched, "Master!"

"Master isn't home. Please leave a message at the beep."

Smirking, Lev dragged the young demon back to the ground. Though the creature clawed at him, Lev held its throat, willing the ephemeral fire to life. It swiftly engulfed the demon, burning the outer shell that housed it. Wildly flailing, the demon landed several blows to Lev's face, but Lev refused to relinquish his grip. Blocking out the mindless screams, Lev waited until the body began to disintegrate. Finally, he dropped the burning carcass and turned to Simael.

"One less to deal with."

"Yeah, we won't see him again for a couple hundred years." Simael grinned as he looked over the small burning piles in the alley. No more than dust would remain when the fires died.

"There are still more out tonight." Lev started walking down the street lined with abandoned buildings. He felt the small groups of humanity huddled within some of them, but his fight wasn't with them.

"Job security," Simael joked as he walked alongside Lev.

Prowling the dark streets, Lev sensed a far stronger

taint than he'd previously encountered. The rational part of him hesitated, knowing he needed additional help and someone more powerful than his trainee. The presence burned over his skin like acid. It would probably be the master of those they'd destroyed.

Lev could tell by Simael's pained expression the other angel could feel it as well. "I want you to return to the central haven, Simael. You've earned a rest."

"But Lev..." Then he sighed and nodded.

As soon as Simael was gone, Lev continued on his self-imposed crusade. Honing in on the invisible trail, Lev began to track it to its source. Whatever it was, it had walked the street less than hour ago. Turning down one of the alleys, Lev ignored a group of men lounging near an open doorway. Though a lone man traveling through their territory would have normally been accosted, the young men did nothing more than watch Lev before they returned to their dealings.

Moving deeper into the warren of alleyways, Lev picked up the smaller taint of nearby imps. He dispatched them easily before any even realized he was near. Taking to the air, Lev rose above the buildings to get a better sense of the demon's trail. Instinct drew him toward the west, past the run-down section of the city. Below him, the city sprawled into an upper class suburb, but Lev knew the demon wasn't there. The signature trail lead him farther west to an area of gated mansions nestled against a mountainside. Rich and powerful, Lev thought. It would explain the overwhelming taint still crawling over his senses.

Carefully, Lev descended closer to the houses. There were very few homes on the long, winding street. It made his job all that much easier. As he focused on each, the largest one drew him like a magnet. Surveying the estate, he saw the mortal guards protecting it. None knew the nature of the one they worked for, so Lev turned his attention to the house itself. He could feel the trace effects of the demon, alone in one of the upper rooms. Cornering a lone demon in its lair would be no real problem. Lev sensed the stronger vibration of power, but it was one he could deal with himself.

Insuring his presence remained shielded, Lev dropped toward the house and through the outer wall. The moment he entered, Lev realized he was too late. The full impact of power rushed over him. No ordinary demon, it had kept its own power hidden until Lev appeared.

Lev stared into the fathomless green eyes of the demon from behind a cage of pure energy. The bars held the angel imprisoned in a barrier he couldn't break. A cruel twist of the demon's lips gave lie to the beauty of the androgynous face. This creature was one of Lucifer's, once a general of the army of the fallen.

"Vical."

"So you know my name, angel." Lazily sprawled in an overstuffed chair, the demon eyed Lev with considerable amusement.

Lev lifted his hand and pushed against the dazzling barrier. It didn't singe his flesh, but the pain burned through him, forcing him to snatch back his hand.

"Foolish enough to come here by yourself..." When Vical trailed off, Lev felt the push of power the demon exerted in a breathless rush into his head. "Lev. A very interesting name. Hebrew for heart."

⊗

By the time Alael reached Vical's mansion, his rage had reached new levels. Tearing through the house, he left nothing but destruction in his wake. He'd known the moment Lev had been captured. Vical's surge of triumph rippled through the astral thread connecting all of his kind.

"Vical!" Alael roared, breaking down the door to the demon's study.

"Well, well..." Vical sat in an overstuffed chair, a goblet dangling from his right hand. "Come to see my new toy?" He waved nonchalantly at the crumpled, feathered form lying in the bottom of the cage.

"He's mine," Alael snarled.

One eyebrow rose and Vical stood slowly. "Oh, is that so?"

Alael circled. Vical followed every step, taunting him. The goblet hitting the floor was the only warning Alael had before Vical slammed him back against the wall, claws digging into his skin.

"How the mighty have fallen," Vical purred. "Is his blood as sweet as it smells? Does he scream your name when you're fucking him?"

Getting his hands between them, Alael shoved Vical away and, with a focus of his power, sent the demon spiraling through the air and crashing through the opposite wall. A general Vical might be, but even he couldn't fight against one of the Order of Blood. "He's mine," Alael growled again.

Ignoring the pain, he tore down the bars holding Lev prisoner. As he picked up the angel, Alael paid no heed to the shrieks of the lesser demon, demanding retribution. He didn't know why he was so drawn to Lev...but he would be damned if anyone else was going to touch Lev before he could.

☙

Alael had freed him from a very bad situation. Eventually Lev would have been able to free himself, but not before a great deal more pain had been inflicted on him. After healing him, Alael had gently laid Lev on the angel's bed and left without a word. Uncertain of why Alael was bent on helping him, Lev had stared silently at the demon the whole time.

Back at home, Lev felt the whispers reaching for him, trying to pull him to the demon. No good would come of him answering the summons.

For several nights after that, Lev stayed as far away as he could from Alael. Returning to the realm of his Order's training grounds, Lev kept himself busy with the tasks of preparing the new ones for their duties. Yet his mind wasn't truly focused on the work. Twice now Alael had gone out of his way to help. It made absolutely no sense except for some warped ulterior motive understood only by the demon himself.

What had been between them must be forgotten. Although relations between angels and demons weren't unknown, it would cause more problems than Lev wanted to handle. His duty was and had always been the welfare of humanity in the first world of the universe. Alael had already proven his own ability to create disorder in the world Lev had to protect.

Finally, on the fourth night, Lev returned to his apartment and crawled wearily into his bed. Normally he didn't need to sleep, but he had the ability to use sleep to re-energize. After having spent the last three days training and nights hunting, he really did need a break. He stretched out naked beneath the sheet. The night was warm, and he'd left the balcony door open for any breeze to circulate through the room. His stream of consciousness slowly faded, pulling him into sleep.

Chapter Three

Alael swore to himself that he wouldn't go, that he could stay away from the angel. Trouble was, that was a lie, and he knew it. He felt it crystal clear every time Lev called out into the ether for him. It was as if a part of him was screaming, tugging him back. This wasn't supposed to happen. But...before he really knew what he was doing, Alael found himself perched on Lev's balcony, leaning against the doorframe as he watched the angel sleep.

Even in his sleep, part of Lev's essence cried out for its twin. Alael knew Lev simply didn't realize what he was doing, that awake the angel had been too busy trying to deny everything. Alael saw his closer presence made Lev's body shift restlessly on the bed. A low sound came from Lev's throat, though he didn't quite awaken. Alael felt the part of the angel needing the connection with him grow quiet as it began to feed on him. Lev seemed completely and utterly defenseless in sleep, and to a degree he was.

Unable to resist, Alael made his way to the bed, stripping as he went. He shuddered when he felt the pull—an intense tug on his very psyche that made it nearly impossible to be away from the angel before him.

As he crawled onto the bed, he pulled the sheet off of Lev, taking care not to wake him. He knelt between Lev's legs, parting them slowly as he leaned forward. With only a small touch of thought, he summoned the shadows, smiling as the smoky, dark tendrils wound around the sleeping angel's wrists and ankles. With Lev bound to the bed, Alael rose on his knees to gaze down at the feast spread before him.

The demon's presence seemed to keep the angel in a state of calm until slowly something impinged on Lev as the shadows pulled at his arms and legs. His eyes opened then blinked sleepily as he tried to fully awaken.

"Shh," Alael purred, sliding his lips over Lev's chest. Closing his mouth over one of Lev's nipples, he rolled it in his teeth, tugging gently. He slid his hand down Lev's body to cup his balls, letting the heat of his blood seep into Lev's skin.

Lev's eyes widened at the sight of Alael kneeling above him. Frantically, he tugged at the restraints even as he felt the heat course over him and through him. Lev couldn't stifle the groan of need, though he tried to free himself from the situation. "Alael, stop, now."

"And if I refuse?" Alael lifted his head. Red eyes bright with pure need stared down at Lev. He rolled Lev's balls in his palm, sliding a finger lower to massage the soft skin just behind them.

Unable to stop the buck of his hips toward Alael's touch, Lev tried to reason with the demon, despite the smoldering fire awakening in his body. "You can't. We can't."

"But we are." Alael pushed his tongue into Lev's mouth, silencing any further protests. He circled the angel's hole, pressing the tip of his finger in just enough to torment and tease. "I want you. I fucking need you."

Giving in to Alael proved far too easy. He rocked his hips, trying to drive the demon's finger deeper into him. He felt the beginning flicker of the raging inferno to come, and everything in him craved it. He bit at Alael's tongue as the demon's words sank into his mind.

Growling into the kiss, Alael pushed Lev's legs apart and ground down on him, driving their cocks together. Too many clothes. Alael was still wearing entirely too many clothes. He pulled away and stood, undressing as quickly as possible.

"You have a choice," he said as he stroked his cock. "Either give me something slick, or make do with my tongue up your ass to ease the way."

Lev really didn't care how Alael took him. The shadows restrained his ankles, keeping him fully exposed to the demon. As his gaze dropped to Alael's hand, a soft whimper escaped Lev. "I need you. Please." Lev knew he was begging, but it didn't matter. He wanted the raging heat to consume him until he knew nothing but Alael.

With a nod from Alael, the shadows binding Lev disappeared. Alael crawled back onto the bed and slid down Lev's body, tracing a line from the angel's navel to his cock with his tongue. A trail of blazing heat followed in his wake and spread over Lev's torso, enveloping the smooth skin in fire.

Once freed, Lev's hands sought the warmth of firm flesh, running over Alael's shoulders before tangling in his hair.

"So sweet," Alael purred as he lapped at Lev's cock, drinking down the clear drops that seeped from the tip.

Gasping, Lev arched his hips, trying to thrust into Alael's mouth as the slow burn sank deeper into him. Biting at his lower lip, Lev tried to stop the sounds struggling to escape him. As he stared down at the dark head bent over him, Lev drank in the sight and feeling as it took him over.

Alael slid his mouth down Lev's cock and exhaled, surrounding the hard flesh in pulsing heat. He began sucking, sliding his lips up and down the shaft, teeth grazing the sensitive skin. Slipping his hands under Lev's thighs, he pushed the angel's legs up to his chest, spreading him wide open.

Without thought, Lev grabbed his legs and held them against his chest, letting Alael position him any way he liked. Lev wanted and needed everything from the demon. A low groan tore from his throat as his body twisted. Living fire began to swallow him, and he released his legs to claw at the sheets beneath.

"Mine." Alael whispered the word over Lev's cock as he let it slip from his mouth. Tilting up Lev's body, he sank down to lick around the angel's hole, sucking on the puckered skin.

Shaking his head as if in denial, Lev gasped as Alael's

tongue probed him. He wrapped his hands around the backs of his legs once more and pulled his hips up to give the demon full access. Sensation after heated sensation raced through him, drawing Lev deeper into the beckoning heat that threatened to take him over. Lev craved it now, and a low, demanding growl broke free of his throat.

As the thickness of Alael's tongue entered him, Lev cried out. The demon was indeed taking him over, and the angel let him. He wanted to know the pain and pleasure of Alael, to feel it all for himself. "Deeper. Harder."

Alael plunged his tongue deep inside Lev's body, groaning as the musky scent and taste of the angel hit him full-force. He fucked Lev with it, thrusting his tongue in and out, sucking on the ring of muscle. His own cock was as hard as a diamond, as painful as it was demanding.

If the angel wanted it then Alael wasn't one to refuse such a request. Tongue buried in Lev's ass, Alael willed it to lengthen and grow. He felt it sliding deeper, its width expanding to stretch the angel open. Reaching up, he wrapped a hand around Lev's cock and started pumping his fist up and down the shaft.

As the tongue filled him, Lev impaled himself harder. With each exquisite rub over his prostate, Lev shuddered as he fucked both the demon's tongue and hand.

Outside, the rumble of thunder signaled a coming storm. A sharp crack of thunder joined Lev's cries when it all became too much. As he screamed the demon's name, the spasms of his own release crashed over him. The sharper, more persistent sensations kept his body shaking with the dual orgasm.

Alael eased out his tongue, willing it back to its original size and length before sliding up to lick Lev clean. The sharp, bittersweet salt of Lev's seed burst on Alael's tongue, dragging a low, hungry growl from deep within his chest. In one swift motion, he thrust his cock deep inside the angel and crushed his mouth to Lev's, feeding the last of the angel's come back to him. Hips slamming against Lev's ass, Alael fucked him hard and fast, setting a brutal rhythm.

Barely given time to recover, Lev wrapped his legs tightly around Alael's waist. The higher position allowed for a deeper penetration, and the pain only excited Lev all the more. Hungrily, he tasted himself on the demon and returned the kiss as his hands ran over Alael's back, nails clawing into his flesh. The demon would drive him insane with need and lust. Part of Lev knew that, but he couldn't help it. The ruthless pounding of the demon's body into his kept him captive.

"Mine!" Alael broke the kiss abruptly. "Say it!" The savage, unrelenting way he thrust into Lev made it crystal clear that he expected an answer.

There was still a part of Lev refusing to submit. Lev shook his head wildly back and forth against the pillow, trying not to let the intensity completely swallow him. The line of his body strained to the bruising jar of Alael's hips as his hands curled around the demon's forearms. Tremors began and quickly spread, tensing his entire

42

body. A pained half-groan, half-growl came from him.

Alael grabbed Lev's arms and pinned them above his head. "Don't...fucking...resist...me!"

A raging heat poured through Lev, driving the words even deeper into him. It didn't stop at the surface; it entangled within him. He knew what the demon wanted, but Lev didn't want to give it. His whole body arched toward Alael as shuddering overtook him. Lev cried out. Tears fell freely down his cheeks as a hard, fast orgasm pulsed through him and rendered him incapable of thought and voice.

Letting out a roar that vibrated the walls, Alael came, filling Lev's body with liquid fire meant to sear him from the inside out. And then he was gone.

The agonizing, internal pain left Lev screaming as he clutched at empty air.

C3

A month. An entire fucking month.

Alael had taken to growling at anyone and everyone whenever he was out. He no longer gave a damn about fucking with mortals. Let them all die and rot—that was his personal opinion on the matter. The fucking pain was sharp and intense, flaring whenever he even so much as thought about Lev. And to make matters worse, one of the fucking angel's former students—Simael—had taken a particular interest in him.

As he sat on the edge of a roof staring down at the people milling about outside one of the many nightclubs on this street, Alael realized he was yet again being watched. Or hunted, as it were. Little puny fuck of an angel was persistent, if anything.

Growling, Alael took off again, determined to get away before he flat out killed the little feathered prick.

When Alael suddenly appeared in his own bedroom, waves of fury emanated from him. Lev stood waiting.

"What the fuck are you doing here?" Alael growled and paced, eyes blazing red, unforgiving. Every time he looked at Lev, all Alael felt was a volatile mix of need, rage and confusion.

The agitated outstretch of the angel's wings stirred a breeze in the room. "I'm here to talk," Lev said. "About Simael."

In two long strides Alael crowded Lev against the wall, so close he tasted the fear in the angel. It only served to anger him further. "He's your fucking student," Alael snarled. "Call him off. Or so fucking help me, I'll rip those pretty wings off his back and shove 'em down his throat."

Lev's hands flew to Alael's shoulders, his fingers gripping the demon's shirt, holding him as he felt the bruising press of Alael's body. Yet Lev stood his ground.

"Simael can't hurt you, Alael. We both know that. He's been ordered to back off already." It was paramount to get Alael to understand before the situation got any worse.

"For his sake, I hope so." Alael crushed his mouth to

Lev's, forcing his tongue inside as he rocked against Lev's body. Planting a hand on the wall on either side of Lev's head, Alael was a wall of solid muscle, completely unmovable.

This wasn't what he'd come here for, or so Lev tried to tell himself. Then why was he melting against the demon with one kiss? His fingers flexed in Alael's shirt before he made the attempt to shove him away. Turning his head, he broke off the kiss, attempting to regain a semblance of sanity. "Not this time, Alael."

"You would deny me again?" As Alael stepped back, the building itself seemed to groan around them. "You would deny the truth?"

Lev had to force himself not to step toward Alael. There was no truth when it came to them. Pain flared and Lev closed his eyes to hide himself. Shaking his head was the only thing he could do.

"You're not here just to talk about your star pupil, are you?"

"That is why I came here."

A knowing smile crept across Alael's lips and he moved closer once more. "Is it now?" He stroked the back of his fingers down Lev's cheek. Where there had been rage before, there was now only tenderness. "Then tell me you don't want me. If it's all you came here for then walk away."

Lev opened his mouth, determined to do just that, but found himself tipping his head, rubbing his cheek against Alael's fingers. Being prey to the demon's mood swings was frustrating to say the least. Lev could barely keep up with him. Still Lev found he wanted the demon's touch too much. He groaned low in his throat as he closed his eyes again. His body already felt like it was on fire, and Alael really hadn't done anything yet.

"I need you, Lev," Alael whispered across Lev's lips. "Being without you hurts too much." Sliding his fingers through Lev's hair, he moved his mouth slowly over Lev's cheek to his ear. "I am a part of you. And you are a part of me."

Lev knew Alael spoke the truth. He would have known a lie. Something was different, though, and Lev sensed it. There was nothing of Alael's normal, more forceful manner. Opening his eyes, Lev studied Alael, seeking the fuller truth. He cupped Alael's cheek with his palm. What he saw inside Alael was his undoing.

"Everything hurts without you."

"I don't know what's going on. I don't know anything other than hunger, anger, pain and sex," Alael said. Resting his forehead against Lev's, he closed his eyes slowly. "What I do know is that I can't go on without you."

Lev pressed his lips pressed tenderly to Alael's, and he brushed his thumbs over Alael's eyelids. "I am your heart, Alael."

For the first time, Lev did understand, and with that understanding came his faith as well.

"I'm sorry," Alael murmured. "I tried to run from it before, but I can't anymore, Lev."

"I didn't know. I didn't look deep enough." Lev drew

Alael's head to his throat. "There's no more running for either of us. Not anymore."

"Please," Alael whispered, sliding his mouth over Lev's neck. "I need to feel you...everywhere."

With a gentle push, Lev nudged Alael toward the demon's bed. "You were right. I belong to you. I was made for you, from you. Just as you were made for me, from me."

When he hit the pallet, Alael laid down, pulling Lev down with him. Shifting beneath the angel, he spread his legs, letting Lev settle between them. He licked a path from Lev's neck to his ear then down to his mouth. The words sat on the tip of his tongue, but every time he tried to tell Lev what he'd finally come to realize, the words wouldn't come. A soft whimper—sounding foreign even to his own ears—escaped Alael, and he rocked his body against Lev's.

"Shh. I already know, Alael. Our souls are one."

The words came from his heart and echoed within his soul as it joined with its twin. Lev began to undress Alael before shrugging out of his own clothing. Quickly, he returned to the demon, his body stretching over Alael's, pressing the demon down onto the pallet.

To Alael, it felt as if something that was broken was finally made whole. For the first time in his existence, he felt something positive—something so strong that it left him breathless and shaking. Clinging to Lev, Alael finally understood.

"Our souls are one." He chanted it over and over,

breathing it into Lev's ear.

Lev was the healing force to Alael's darkness. Sometime he might explain the meaning of his name to the demon, if Alael didn't know it already. The press of Lev's lips silenced them both as Lev captured the demon's mouth in a breath-stealing kiss.

Wrapping his legs around Lev's waist, Alael surged upward, sliding their bodies together. He cupped Lev's head and deepened the kiss, filling the angel's mouth with soft sounds of need and want and love.

The angel's wings flattened to surround them both, shielding them from the outside world. Alael was truly his, and Lev's heart soared in the knowledge. He could feel everything within the demon, and it resonated to his core. Ending the kiss, he wet his hand and ran it slowly over his own cock. A small shift of his hips positioned his body, and a slow forward thrust drove him inside the demon. His eyes darkened, taking on a heated intensity as he whispered, "You are my soul. Forever mine."

"Yes." Eyes rolling back and closing, Alael opened himself completely, drowning in the light of Lev's soul— their soul. Every stroke Lev made caused the light to pulse and grow, spreading through Alael, coiling around the fires within him.

In that, Lev understood he belonged to Alael as well. There couldn't be one without the other. It played serious havoc with the balance. Their bond had already formed and consumed them both, just as it was doing now. The expression of his love came from his body, heart, mind and their soul. Slowly he drew Alael upward with each grinding rock and thrust that joined them as one body. "I am your soul. Forever yours, Alael."

Alael shuddered suddenly, eyes locking onto Lev's then widening. "Lev!"

Lev watched the changing expression of surprise, pleasure and surrender in Alael's face as the demon shook beneath him in his release. It was what he craved from his demon. Even as his body quickened its rhythm, Lev's mind dwelt on those two words, and he whispered them softly, "My demon."

He closed his eyes. A sudden hard driving force held his body captive to the demon's as his own release swept through him. When Lev started to relax from the intensity, a depthless well of emotions surged through Lev to flood Alael.

Alael rocked beneath him, chanting Lev's name. Clinging to Lev, the demon trembled, shocked to the core. Despite his dark heart, his undoing had been at the hands of an angel.

"Do you even understand what is between us, Alael?"

Blinking up at him, Alael nodded. "I have no words for it, but I can't deny the peace my soul feels."

Content the demon understood, Lev rested his head on Alael's shoulder. The twin rhythms of their beings twined as one, binding them as one soul in two bodies. As it was always meant to be.

ANGELS OF BLOOD

Chapter One

"He must be destroyed!" Chancellor Brahm slammed both hands onto the dark wooden table, the sound thundering throughout the cavernous room. "He is dangerous, out of control!"

"Irael is not to be destroyed." All eyes shifted to the man standing in the doorway, his own gaze pale but sharp. He strode into the room, ignoring the whispers.

Chancellor Brahm looked him up and down. "And you are?"

"Adon," the man said simply. He came to a stop a few feet from the massive round table that dominated the room.

"Adon is..." Lord Eralin looked at the others before continuing, "...the Commander of the Chaos Order."

The chancellor's eyes widened and he dropped into his seat. "I thought they were a myth," he muttered.

Lord Eralin snorted. "Hardly. They are simply covert in their operations, Chancellor, but I assure you they are very much real."

"Yes, I see." Chancellor Brahm took in the commander's form. Skin the color of ebony stretched taut over a muscular frame. Adon's hair, white as a virgin's robes, was pulled back, and his eyes... Sweet gods, the dark angel's eyes were mesmerizing. Dangerous. Brahm swallowed hard, resisted the urge to lick his lips. Here was beauty and death encased in black flesh.

"Chancellor Brahm." That voice—commanding even at rest. "I have experience in dealing with Irael. I will gladly bring him under control."

Brahm could only nod, gaze riveted to the tap of one long finger on the vicious whip coiled at the Commander's left hip. "Yes."

ᘓ

A hooded gaze swept over the marbled hall before it settled on one particular individual. Irael gestured for Mian to come closer.

The bone raven near the angel momentarily paused in its voracious feasting, its wickedly curved beak gleaming with blood. Irael ran his hand over the black feathers on its head as he watched Mian scuttle toward him.

"Where is our entertainment, Mian? I expect them to arrive soon to amuse my guests."

Mian threw himself prostrate on the floor. "They will be here. I promise." Daring to lift his head, he added, "The Naal are outside the gates, rounding up the denizens."

"For your sake, I hope they return, and soon."

Mian stared at the deceptively fragile beauty of the man sitting regally in his chair. All knew, despite his fair, angelic appearance, the blackest heart beat within the breast of their god.

Like an answer to the darkest prayer, the throne room doors opened and the Naal marched in, misshapen hands clutching arms and legs, dragging some of the less enthusiastic participants across the black stone floor. Many screamed, flailing wildly, desperation setting in when expectant, hungry growls met their cries.

Mian let out the breath he didn't know he'd been holding. He kept his gaze riveted to the spectacle before them, allowing the slightest bit of gratitude to seep out in a sigh of relief.

The beasts grew hungrier, waiting impatiently to be fed. One of the Ektih tried repeatedly to break free and get to the crowd outside its cage. The flap of its leathery red wings beat against the barrier and its long beak snapped as if trying to cut through what held it.

A small wave of Irael's hand expanded the confines of the individual cages, making them one. As he nodded, his Naal began tossing in their captives.

Men and women alike screamed, their faces twisted in masks of horror as they prepared to fight for their lives within the cages. The beasts didn't outright attack. Most preferred their prey still breathing. They enjoyed the hunt. There was nowhere to hide as each beast chose its meal for the evening.

When the first Ektih made its catch, the crowd roared its approval. Thunderous applause filled the room as the beast's beak broke through its victim's skull, the long tongue siphoning the brain matter out as the man convulsed beneath it.

Mian swallowed hard, barely able to stop the trembling. Though he was one of Irael's personal servants, he was still a lesser revenant. If he displeased his god, this too would be his fate.

All around the hall circling the cages, his guests straightened in their seats in avid appreciation of the treat they were witnessing.

One of the Naal dragged his captive up the steps of the massive platform where a priest waited to sacrifice the woman for the pleasure of their god.

When one of the hapless victims narrowly escaped the snapping jaws of an Astas, the crowd cheered as wildly as they had when a ferocious Sitil devoured one of the prisoners. Amused by the spectacle, Irael motioned for one of the Naal to throw the man a spear.

The man scrambled for the weapon and held it at length, the determination to survive fierce in his expression. When the Astas lunged for him, the man caught it and impaled the sinewy body on the weapon. The crowd cheered for him as he shoved the beast away.

Rather impressed despite the original intention he'd had for the fellow, Irael watched the untrained but effective fighter. As a Staras began stalking the young man, Irael straightened in his chair, curious to see what they both would do.

Warily, the man danced around the beast twice his height, barely missing the lash of its black tail. As it moved closer, he jabbed at it with the spear, catching the tip against the beast's muzzle. An enraged roar filled the room, blending with the screams of the dying.

Not expecting its meal to fight, the Staras reared on its hind legs to intimidate its prey. A quick thrust from the spear drew more blood. Furious, the beast crashed down, trapping the man beneath it. Lowering its snout, the Staras revealed dual rows of razor-sharp teeth. It seemed as if the beast was smiling. Then it snapped, severing the man's head from his shoulders with the sheer force of its bite.

With the last of the victims dying, the crowd began to lull, returning to their feast. Eventually the Naal dragged the remaining captives out of the throne room toward the dungeons. The beasts feasted as well, devouring their meals in the cages.

CB

The heavy weight of Irael's gaze fell on his servant, Mian, as he came into the room. His steps seemed to slow until he threw himself on the floor in front of Irael.

"What is it now, Mian?" Irael regarded him with little favor. He knew damn well that whatever Mian had to tell him, he didn't want to hear.

Keeping his forehead to the hard marble, Mian

mumbled, "My god, there is someone in the outer chamber wanting to see you."

"And who someone would that be?"

Before Mian could answer, the doors of the throne room opened. Mian let out a terrified squeak, scurrying out of the way as the visitor started toward the dais. Although he was concealed beneath a black robe with a deep hood, it was clear from the stature alone that this visitor was a man. When he reached the dais, he stopped, but did not bow.

"You are under investigation by the Chaos Order," the man said simply, not removing his hood.

"And this impresses me how?" Irael shot a dark look at Mian. He wasn't pleased with his servant's behavior. Rising from his throne, Irael drawled, "Mian, I suggest you make yourself absent before I feed you to Brmol."

As Mian hastily vacated the room, the beady gaze of the bone raven followed him.

"Irael, you have been charged with cruelty, torture, and murder. If I find any evidence of such during my stay here, you will be brought before the Universal Council to face trial and sentence." The man swept back his hood. "And they won't be as gentle on you as I am."

"I am to expect gentleness from you, Adon? Have you changed that greatly?" Amused, Irael stilled in front of him. "And exactly what kind of evidence are you looking for? Murder not sanctioned by the Council? You'll probably find plenty of that here."

"I do not recall an ounce of complaint when my whip

tasted your flesh," Adon whispered as he began circling Irael. "Tell me, Irael. Do you still bear my marks?"

Stepping back abruptly, Irael hissed out a warning. "What has that to do with your investigation? If the Council has just complaint, the cowards need to face me themselves."

"I am the Council," Adon snarled. "And you did not answer my question. Have you forgotten your place so quickly, pup?"

Irael's wings outstretched in a threatening stance as he stood his ground. His normally short nails began to lengthen, resembling razor sharp talons. "Since you don't seem to recall, I had no place to forget, Adon."

The robe fell to the floor and black-feathered wings spread out. Adon's smile was anything but warm. "You have forgotten." He tapped the coiled whip, the smile turning sinister. "Perhaps a reminder is in order."

It required every ounce of will Irael had to stop himself from reacting to the sight of his former master. Bristling in agitation, he refused to fall to his knees. Instead he turned his back on Adon and approached his throne. "Nothing is in order, Adon. If you haven't noticed, it never has been."

In a split second, the snap of Adon's whip reverberated throughout the throne room. It coiled around Irael's throat and, with a hard jerk, Adon had Irael's back against him.

"You never learn, pup."

Growling sharply with the pain, Irael tore at the

leather strap, trying to get it off his throat. Slashing at his own skin, his sharp talons cut deep into his flesh. "Back off, Adon!"

Adon's forked tongue traced the curve of Irael's ear. "You've not changed," he whispered. "You still crave this." Another snap of his wrist and the whip left Irael's throat, moving as if the leather were a living thing, retreating to Adon's hand.

Bleeding from his self-inflicted wounds, Irael refused to react by either word or action. Focusing a minute amount of energy, he began to heal himself.

Adon tipped Irael's head and licked the blood from the side of his neck. Growling low, he said, "I expect my chambers to be ready at once and will take my meals there. I will sit in on your sessions."

Biting hard at his lower lip only drew more blood. Irael clenched his hands into fists at his sides. "It will be done, Adon."

"Very good." Adon released him and stepped back.

Slowly turning to face him, Irael narrowed his eyes. "I would prefer that those in the Council who have a problem with me face me personally. I already know that's not likely since they are cowards. Or have you been gone so long from them that you don't see it all for what it is?"

Adon snaked an arm around Irael's waist and pulled him close, his lips just a breath from Irael's. "The Council matters nothing to me. Do you really think that is my only reason for being here?"

Even wanting to find the energy to break away was

damn near impossible. Why did Adon still affect him? Shielding his expression, Irael let nothing of his thoughts show. "Why else would you be here?"

"To reclaim what is mine." Without giving Irael a chance to answer, Adon captured him in an enslaving kiss, forcing his tongue into Irael's mouth.

Without thought, Irael opened to Adon and the familiar longing spread like wild fire through him. Adon's kisses had been so rare when they'd been together, but Irael had never forgotten the feel or taste. His knees threatened to buckle as the forked tongue devoured him.

Adon pulled back slowly, licking Irael's lips. "I expect you in my chambers immediately." With that, he stepped around Irael to follow Mian out of the room.

Irael's first preservative instinct was to disobey the order as he watched Adon walk away. Yet the movement of Adon's body fascinated him. The dark angel wore only tight pants and a leather harness strapped across his chest and back, leaving little to the imagination. Catching himself, Irael frowned heavily as the door closed, cutting off his view.

Irael went to his own private rooms, arguing vehemently with himself. He neither wanted nor needed the complication Adon brought back into his life.

Duty had meant everything to Adon, and Irael doubted that had changed. Duty had taken Adon from him the last time and left Irael under the "protection" of the Council. That had degenerated to nothing more than being treated as the basest creature in existence until he'd escaped and forcefully carved out his own life on this planet. He already knew none of the Council would have dared tell Adon the truth.

Even the vast space of his rooms made Irael near claustrophobic, and his mind gave him no peace. With a determined stride, he headed toward the tower stairs, climbing them to the roof. Stepping out, he stared at the vast expanse of sky and dragged in a refreshing breath. Near the ledge, he sat on the stone, legs dangling over the edge as his gaze swept the landscape. Cruel he might be at times, but it was a necessity that stopped criminals from preying on the weak. When he'd arrived on this planet, the people didn't even have the rudiments of education. Yet under his guidance, three cities had risen.

Those were things Irael would never bother explaining. He knew the truth and had little care for others' accusations. Of course, he didn't have the Council's permission to do any of this and he paid them no allegiance.

"You did not come."

Irael didn't even turn to look at him. "Did you really expect me to, Adon? You're not my master anymore."

"Why did you leave? I came back for you, but the Council told me you'd left." Adon brushed Irael's hair from his neck, following with a kiss as soft as a whisper.

"I left because I had to." Thankfully he didn't shiver beneath the drifting touch. Irael couldn't hide the underlying bitterness, no matter how hard he tried, and it seeped into his words. "And now you are here because they sent you to deal with me. How like them."

"They didn't send me." Gripping Irael's chin, Adon turned Irael's head to face him. "I interrupted the Council when I received word they were planning your destruction. I gave them no choice in the matter."

Irael plastered a blank look on his features. "Destroy me? For what? Cruelty without their permission?" Surprised by Adon's admission, Irael allowed a bit of a smile to crack through the façade. "How like you to force the matter on them. I should have known."

"I've spent three hundred years looking for you," Adon whispered, thumb sliding over Irael's lips. "I've lost you." For the briefest moment, sadness flickered in his eyes before Adon blinked it away. He released Irael reluctantly and stood to walk away.

Chapter Two

Instantly confused, Irael slowly turned to face him. "Why would it even matter to you, Adon? Duty always mattered more to you, and just as you should, you've always done your duty."

Adon stopped, his back to Irael. "I learned long ago what was important. I told them I would bring you under control, under the condition of my leave from service."

"Leave? Why would you leave?" Though surprised, Irael still viewed Adon with a great deal of suspicion. The angel had always been a creature of the Order. Adon lived and breathed for it. Nothing had ever stood in the way of devotion and duty.

Adon walked to the opposite side of the tower roof and leaned against the stone crenellation. "I left for you."

"For me? Forgive me if I sound disbelieving, Adon, but after all this time, it's rather hard to believe."

Adon spun around and rushed Irael, jerked him to his feet and slammed him back against the tower wall, Irael's shirt fisted in his hands. "Hard to believe?" he snapped. "I've not slept since we separated! I've had no peace, Irael. Every breath I take is infused with your scent, every morsel of food tastes like your body, your blood, every thought is invaded with memories of you. I came here without the intention of leaving!"

Irael's voice rose as well. "You left because you were ordered to do so! I had nothing to do with it. Since you are not leaving, you are here to rule my world for the Council. Is that it, Adon? I have no hope of fighting you. You could kill me easily. The war would be over before it even started."

"I came here because I love you!"

That silenced Irael as he tried to decipher the truth for himself. For a long moment he didn't say anything. What meaning could he take from the words? Irael wasn't sure anymore, though he desperately wanted to believe Adon. "I trusted you once before until everything turned to ashes around me. I was nothing to the ones you left me with."

Adon released him and turned away. "I thought you would be safe," he said quietly. "I trusted them to keep you safe. No one would tell me anything other than that you had left."

"They hated me because they thought I weakened you. Didn't they tell you I destroyed their precious temple after they tried to have me killed? I was and always will be a threat to them." Irael headed for the door to return to his chambers.

"They told me nothing." Adon met Irael's gaze before Irael stepped through the door.

"I belong to the Faction of the Disillusioned, Adon.

Yes, in the eyes of one like you, I have fallen that far. Now how much do you love me?" Without waiting for an answer, Irael descended the steps.

Adon didn't hesitate; he followed him. "More than life itself, Irael. Enough to give up everything."

Once inside his room, Irael turned to face Adon, folding his arms across his chest. His wings twitched in agitation. "How is it that I can say such a thing and you don't even flinch? The man I knew would have flown into a rage and beaten me within an inch of my life for even daring to say the name."

Adon's ebony skin was a stark contrast to the pristine white of the room. Running a fingertip over the smooth, white surface of the table beside him, he said, "Perhaps because I've become disillusioned myself. Without you, nothing else matters."

Curiosity and something else he refused to admit made Irael approach Adon. "Have you changed so much?" Part of Irael wanted to believe what he was being told; the other half shied away from any notion of placing himself in the same situation as before.

Adon looked up at him, gaze almost pleading. "I would do anything for you. If you told me to go...then I would go." Adon closed his eyes, took a deep breath and knelt on the floor before Irael. "Anything."

Disbelieving shock held Irael immobile. He knew what the gesture meant. Crouching down in front of Adon, he asked, "You know what will happen if the Council finds out you are here like this. They're expecting you to bring me back under their thumb."

"I would die for you," Adon said without moving from his position.

Sighing, Irael sat heavily on the floor, crossing his legs. "Do you really believe I would do that to you? Leave it to you to come back into my life and turn it completely upside down."

"I need you, Irael. I came here on the hope you'd feel the same."

"It's not that simple anymore. It never really has been. You and I both know it. It has never troubled me to be considered a renegade. But you..." He trailed off as he touched Adon's face.

Adon's eyes closed and he turned his face into the touch, brushing a soft kiss against Irael's fingers. "If...you want me to go..."

"You must return to the Council, Adon. You belong with the Order." Irael drew back his hand before the contact led to painful memories.

"Irael..." Adon stood. "I belong nowhere if not with you."

For the first time, Irael regretted that he hadn't stayed where he'd been put. "Then you will give the Council a puppet."

"I give the Council nothing. I give you everything." Adon looked away. A moment passed before he continued. "I am sorry for bothering you, Irael."

The Council could have found no better way to crush

Irael without spilling a drop of their own blood. Irael rose, knowing he would have another regret and probably sooner than he wanted to face it. The moment he touched Adon, the need to connect rushed through him, just as he knew it would. When his lips met Adon's, a soft cry broke free before he could stop it, and Irael desperately sought the taste of his master.

Momentarily surprised, Adon opened to Irael. Desperation began to seep into the kiss, and Adon's arms snaked around Irael's waist, holding him close. Adon walked them back until they reached the wall then he deepened the kiss.

As if he couldn't get enough, Irael held on, sinking beneath the pounding surge of chaotic emotion. A moment later, he sank to his knees in front of Adon, bowing his head. He pulled the tie out of his hair, and the full length of it cascaded around him. "As I once belonged to you, take your pleasure of me." In his heart, Irael begged for one last chance to be given what had once meant everything to him.

Adon reached down and slipped a finger beneath Irael's chin, lifting his head to see his face. "Present yourself to me."

With no more than a thought, the clothing on Irael's body dissolved as he stood and turned to face the wall. Spreading his legs, he raised his arms up and out over his head. His heart beat a frantic rhythm, and the hardness of his cock completely betrayed his need.

Adon approached him and draped Irael's hair over his

right shoulder while pressing a kiss to the left one. "I love you," he whispered. With a flick of his wrist, the whip uncoiled and Adon stepped back. "Are you ready?"

Irael truly hadn't expected that Adon would allow him to feel the kiss of his. A shiver ran through him as he nodded. "Please, Adon, I need to feel it all again."

The only answer was the loud snap of leather cutting through the air. The barbed tip lashed at Irael's back.

When the whip connected with his flesh, Irael jerked, but he held the position, drowning in the warmth of the sharp sting. A trickle of blood ran down his spine.

Another strike created a deeper cut diagonally across Irael's back. Then it all stopped. Breathless seconds passed before Adon licked away the blood and warmth seeped over the abused flesh.

"My Beautiful One," Adon breathed, mouth sliding up Irael's spine. "How I've needed you..."

Adon had been the only one who could draw such an overwhelming and complete response from Irael. Irael's talons clawed the wall. Many of the scars on his back had faded, but they were still visible simply because Irael refused to get rid of them.

"I will taste you, feast on you," Adon whispered, lips drifting along the top of Irael's left shoulder, over the arch of his neck. He shifted and without warning brought the flat of his palm down onto Irael's right buttock, the sound sharp and sweet. "And when I am done, I will take you."

The sound of Adon's voice, his touch, set Irael on fire. Turning his head, Irael tried to get close enough to Adon to taste. All over again, he belonged to the dark angel. The sense of it flowed through his entire being as if they had never been separated.

Another slap landed hard on Irael's ass and Adon hissed in his ear. "Turn. On your knees. I want those lips wrapped around me."

With a fluid twist of his body, Irael went to his knees in front of Adon. Irael raised his gaze to Adon's. The stormy hue of Adon's gray eyes held Irael enthralled, and he knew his own filled with the love and adoration he could never fully hide. Irael wrapped his fingers around the base of Adon's cock as he leaned in, opening his mouth. The first lick of his tongue tasted the sweet drops on his master's skin before he drew Adon's cock fully into his mouth.

Adon rumbled his pleasure, one palm flat against the wall as his other hand rested on Irael's head, fingers moving lower to softly stroke his cheek. "So beautiful..." Adon gasped, fingers tightening on Irael's jaw as he thrust forward, driving his cock into Irael's mouth. "My sweet pup."

Unable to say anything, Irael relied on his actions to do it for him as he worshiped Adon. He swallowed Adon with every thrust of the dark angel's hips, and his fingers caressed Adon's balls.

"Irael..." Adon shuddered, groaned then thrust forward, heat spilling down Irael's throat as he came. Irael drank in every pulse of liquid given to him. When Adon began to calm, the pressure eased as Irael pulled back and settled into his prior position.

Smiling down at him, Adon said, "Now, on the bed, on your back. I wish to taste you."

Irael stood and went to the bed. He rolled to his back and drew up both of his legs, holding onto his thighs. The arch of his ass exposed him fully to Adon's hungry stare.

Adon crawled onto the bed and bent Irael in half, lifting his hips. The position let him see Irael's eyes. Adon's red forked tongue slithered out and flicked over Irael's hole before pushing inside. A dark stormy gaze held Irael captive as Adon's tongue slithered deeper, lengthening as it tasted the depths of his body.

Irael cried out, helpless to stop the sound as his body writhed, rocking against the invasion. Fire blazed through him, the need for Adon surging over him. He would do anything for more. "Adon, fill me. Make me know you again."

As Adon slowly withdrew, he willed his tongue to swell and relax, opening Irael over and over. When he finally slipped free, Adon wet his cock and lowered Irael's hips, pushing deep inside him in one smooth but forceful stroke.

Irael sank beneath the possession of his body. His legs and arms encircled Adon, clinging to him as Irael rocked for his own pleasure and Adon's. "I could never stop dreaming about you. I never will."

Adon settled onto him, taking them both toward a long-needed release. Lips drifting over Irael's, Adon whispered, "You are my soul, Irael. Take me into you, breathe me in." When his mouth covered Irael's, Adon exhaled gently, filling Irael's soul as surely as he filled Irael's body.

The rush flooded him, entwining more deeply within Irael's mind and soul. Something inwardly snapped, leaving Irael incapable of defenses or barriers. Every part of him hurt in that moment, pain beyond the physical, until the power itself filled him enough to quiet it. Open to Adon, Irael shook, the pleasure leaving him breathless even as his body strained to come again.

"Never again will I leave you," Adon murmured.

Without stopping the flow of energy between them, Adon came, filling Irael with his release. Every throb of his body was mirrored in his soul, his breath leaving him as he felt their souls bind. It took several seconds longer for him to stop shaking, and when he did, he dropped his head to Irael's shoulder, eyes closing as his tears wet the pale skin.

"Never again," he whispered.

His own tears flowed with Adon's. Irael trembled uncontrollably. What happened to him? Irael could barely take in the full force of the chaotic connection between them. He couldn't stop his own mental demand for it, either, and absorbed all that was given to him.

After a few moments, Adon kissed Irael's neck softly before pulling out of him. Settling on the bed, he drew Irael close, holding him tight. "I'm so sorry for the past. Please forgive me."

"None of it was your fault, Adon. I knew that a long

time ago. There is nothing to forgive." Irael's voice didn't rise above a whisper. "Looking back, I should have stayed, but none of it worked out as it should have. Not your fault, not my fault."

Adon drew in a deep breath and let it out before kissing Irael's hair. "I don't know if you believe me, but I love you...so much it hurts."

It took Irael a moment to form the words he wanted to say. "I never felt you before. Not like this. I can feel everything of you inside me now."

"As I can you, my Beautiful One. As I can you."

Chapter Three

Irael had left him. It had taken Adon too damn long to awaken, and in that time Irael disappeared. Adon centered himself, focused on the thread connecting his soul to Irael's. When he realized just where the Council had placed Irael, fury surged through Adon's veins. While Irael could not travel through the Abyss, Adon could— he'd been one of the three to create it.

With nothing more than force of will, Adon entered the void. There was nothing but emptiness, darkness swallowing everything like a black hole in space. Focusing inwardly again, he found the thread. The astral cord bound their souls. He could feel Irael's fear thrumming through it. First he must take of those who thought to interfere then he would attend to what was his.

 C3

Irael couldn't connect to anything. It left him in a vacuum of darkness, deprived of sight and sound. Already his thought processes had begun to dissolve into nothing but a mindless fear as he floated within the seemingly unending vastness. Whatever sound he made was lost.

Strong arms encircled him then wings enfolded him, lifting him away. The journey out of the void was almost as terrifying as the journey into it. Yet the arms and wings kept him safe, shielded, until his feet touched solid ground once more.

Irael sank his talons into Adon in a death grip. Mentally nothing had really yet clicked other than the overwhelming desperation that tried to feed on the connection with Adon.

Eyes closed, Adon opened the connection between them, flooding Irael with his energy. His arms and wings tightened around Irael, shielding him from everything else as Adon eased them both down to their knees.

"Feed."

With no real comprehension of where he was or what he was doing, Irael's mind and soul hungrily devoured everything offered to restore his balance. Finally something he could feel outside of himself. Once he started feeding, he couldn't stop. Tears spilled down his cheeks as he clung to Adon.

They remained locked together, Adon's wings enveloping them both, for what seemed like ages. When Adon finally felt Irael's presence in his mind, he tilted Irael's head until frightened blue eyes met his.

Irael had to touch the smooth ebony of Adon's face just to reassure himself the angel was truly there. "I didn't think you would help me."

Adon's eyes closed, the pain of Irael's doubt too much.

He turned his face into the touch, lips brushing a soft kiss across Irael's palm. "I've searched so long for you," he whispered.

"I've destroyed everything for us, Adon. How can you even..."

"Irael..." Adon sighed, shivering whenever Irael touched him. "We're both outlaws now, but as long as you don't leave me again, I don't care. Please don't leave me."

"This isn't what I meant to do to you. I thought you would stay there and run things for the Council." Never in his wildest dreams did Irael think Adon would follow him.

Adon pulled back and stared down at him. "The Council means nothing to me," he said, cupping Irael's face in his hands. "What little there's left of it."

Adon had never been the renegade type, not as much as Irael had been. It seemed Irael had sealed both of their fates, though he'd never meant to drag the angel down with him. "What did you do, Adon?"

"Do you honestly think they willingly told me where you were? You might enjoy my whip, but it seems choice members of the Council did not."

"It's not wise of me to say they were long past deserving it. And it wasn't the smartest thing you've ever done." Irael felt torn. He wanted Adon with him, yet a feeling of guilt accompanied the selfish desire.

"It was necessary. It was them or you."

"What now, Adon? Both of us are on the run. You weren't supposed to free me from that prison. I'm not even sure how you did. But I don't think there's anywhere safe for us."

"We're going underground." Adon stroked Irael's cheek with his fingers, sliding them down to trace his lips. "Back to Tralen. No one but those wishing to hide go there. We can move on whenever we need to. And do not worry about how I freed you. Those answers will come in time."

Irael pressed a kiss to Adon's fingertips before he bowed his head. Everything had come down hard on Irael. Although he was fiercely independent of the Council, he knew Adon wasn't. Resting his forehead on the angel's shoulder, Irael sighed heavily. "Not exactly the life you would want, or what I meant to drag you into."

"Trust me when I say it is a small matter." Adon slipped his fingers beneath Irael's chin, lifting his head. "We are one. Nothing and no one will come between us and live."

"I've destroyed everything and it's a small matter?" If anything, Irael felt completely confused as to why Adon would see it that way. He'd just basically torn Adon from his entire life.

"Do you trust me, Irael?"

"Once I didn't trust you as I should have. Now I do." Pressing his forehead against Adon's, Irael slipped his arms around Adon's neck. "I think I just keep messing everything up."

"Then trust this..." Adon's words trailed off as he brought their mouths together, his tongue seeking entrance.

Irael clung to Adon as his lips parted, accepting the needful kiss. Tears slipped from beneath Irael's eyelids as he acknowledged his own emotional dependence on Adon. Without Adon, he was no more than a mockery of himself. He had already lived that.

The insistent pressure of Adon's body soon had Irael on his back. Adon plundered the depths of his mouth. The kiss was sharp and hungry. Low growls rumbled from deep within Adon as he edged his way between Irael's legs, thrusting against him.

Too much clothing impeded everything Irael wanted. Prone on the ground, he arched up, grinding tightly against Adon as his tongue pushed against his master's, seeking more.

Pulling back to stare down into Irael's eyes, Adon said, "Take what you will."

With a soft growl, Irael rolled them both and pinned the angel beneath him. An aggressive edge fueled the descent of his hands over Adon's body. Their clothing disintegrated into dust with a small exertion of will on Irael's part.

Adon was left bare to the hungry roaming of his hands. Irael's mouth captured his, tongue pushing demandingly between Adon's lips.

Adon groaned and opened to the kiss, tongue fighting with Irael's for control. He drew up his legs, cradling Irael between them. Hands gripping Irael's hips, Adon pushed, grinding their cocks together. "In me," he growled into Irael's mouth.

By coming after him, Adon had revealed the true scope of his own emotional need for Irael, and now Irael wanted it all. Giving Adon no breathing space, Irael slicked his own cock as quickly as he could. The need to possess fueled him. Irael drove his length into the tight resistance of Adon's body. Biting savagely at Adon's lips, Irael raked his nails down Adon's chest before gripping Adon's hips.

Adon jerked and growled. "Take me!" he snapped, fingers digging into Irael's arms.

A quick motion had Adon's hands pinned above his head as Irael held him down. The final hard thrust of his hips buried him deep inside the angel. Not even pausing, the piston of his hips brutally drove into him. Irael stared down at Adon as he took complete possession of the angel.

Adon let out a sound that was something between a roar and moan. He ground his hips tightly against Irael, meeting every hard thrust, gasping as he began to shake.

Seeing Adon writhe helplessly beneath him sent a surge of desire through Irael. Using only one hand to hold the angel's, he closed the other around Adon's cock. The sounds coming from Adon's lips spurred Irael on. With the tight friction, a burning ache settled deep inside Irael and explosively ignited as he thrust one last time and came.

Adon's eyes widened and the world beyond them faded into darkness. Irael's name fell from his lips before Adon's spine arched. Lightning shot through him, through

Irael, the true breadth of Adon's power too strong to hold.

Irael froze as the current fused them together. His eyes widened, his senses failed, leaving him within the surge of power. Collapsing against Adon, Irael convulsed with the immense flood of energy.

Long moments later, the world returned to normal. Adon drew in a sharp breath and held onto Irael's hands, eyes squeezed shut. "Irael…"

Irael could barely move. All he did was moan softly as he heard his name. Slowly, he moved his hands down Adon's chest.

"Irael? Talk to me, please, love," Adon pleaded.

"Who are you?" The overwhelming surge had resembled something Irael had felt within the void. He couldn't make any sense of the influx burning through him.

Adon sighed and caressed Irael's back. "My true name is Adonai. I am one of the Creator angels, and one of the three who created the Abyss."

Sliding off of Adon, Irael sat beside him, trying to take in that particular piece of information. "You're part of the creation."

"I'm one of those responsible for the creation." Adon stared unblinking at Irael. "I created you."

A gentle rain began to fall on them both, cleansing them, but Irael paid it no heed. No words could convey how he felt at that moment. He stared uncomprehendingly at his own hands. "Is that why I am tied to you?"

"Yes...and no. I wanted something special, someone for me. Call it selfishness on my part, call it greed, call it what you will—but that is why I created you, Irael. I created you for me and for me only."

"You didn't tell me. Why?" Blinking rapidly, Irael finally looked at him. "They knew, didn't they? The whole time they knew."

"They did. Why do you think they took you away from me? I kept it quiet, kept it from you, for your safety, though in the end, it didn't matter." Adon looked...defeated...as he spoke, gaze pleading with Irael to understand.

Irael found himself bereft of words. So much could have been avoided. They were both at fault in that; it wasn't just him. "Are all the secrets done, Adon?"

"Yes. I'm sorry. I hoped to keep you safe, and instead I've lost you."

"I understand. We both made very bad mistakes with each other, and we both need to forgive each other. I'm just not sure if we can forgive ourselves." Sighing heavily, Irael leaned down to rub his cheek against the angel's.

"Don't leave me again," Adon whispered. "Please, Irael. I need you too much."

"I'm not going anywhere. Nothing has the right to keep us apart. Not even the Council. They were wrong, and I'm not going to hide from them anymore."

Adon chuckled, relaxing finally. Slipping his hand around the back of Irael's neck, he tugged his lover onto the ground, capturing Irael's mouth in a kiss.

Half-hovering on him, Irael stretched out against Adon. The rhythm of their hearts beat as one, and Irael couldn't deny the truth of his existence. With Adon's kiss, he opened completely, returning the gentle pressure. The tenor of the kiss slowly changed, and Irael answered the growing need he sensed.

Adon's other hand slid down to Irael's hip, holding him close. Then with one graceful movement, he had Irael on his back on the ground. Moving his mouth over Irael's neck, Adon settled between Irael's legs. His wings expanded, fluttered as he kissed his way down Irael's chest, sucking one nipple into his mouth.

In one moment, Irael completely forgot anything and everything except for the angel pinning him down. He stroked the feathery tips of one wing above them.

Adon's growl rolled over Irael's stomach then lower. It deepened seconds before Adon took Irael's cock into his mouth, swallowing it to the root. Hands on Irael's hips, he demanded Irael's pleasure, demanded his release.

Trained too well by Adon, Irael writhed helplessly and his hips thrust upward several times before a tremor shot through him. The demand reached him from Adon's mind, forcing him to respond. Irael spilled down the angel's throat as he cried out.

Adon drank every drop greedily, licking Irael clean when he was done. Sliding back up Irael's body, Adon kissed him hard, sharing the taste. "I will take you far away from here, far away from everything. Then I want you, want to bury myself inside you, hear you screaming my name again."

There wasn't a damn thing in existence Irael could deny Adon. Knowing the angel was his creator only tightened the bonds between them. When he could speak, Irael's voice held the deep-seated need he held for Adon. "Anywhere. I don't care. As long as you're there."

"I will always be there. Always."

UNHOLY NEED

Chapter One

Nichael perched on a tree branch of the old oak and watched the house. The magical energy encasing the house made it difficult for him to see what might be happening behind the closed blinds. He'd already been filled in on the potential danger of the man who lived here. As an angel of the Lower Order of Creation, Nichael had been left the task of deciding the ultimate fate of the mage tinkering with power beyond his understanding.

From across the street, another watched the same house. A black gaze drifted from the house to the oak then back to the house. A slow smile curled the lips holding a cigarette. As he cupped the lighter in front of the cigarette, Nias chuckled low. He took a slow drag and exhaled a moment later, lazily watching the gray smoke drift away in the stiff breeze.

Nichael was already aware of the other presence, and the movement of his wings rustled in faint agitation. Looking toward the street, he unerringly located the demon. Nichael wasn't surprised, but he didn't exactly welcome his fallen brother either.

A flash lit one of the front windows of the house, and Nias grinned. Silly fool of a mortal. Nias dropped the cigarette and ground it out on the sidewalk with the toe of his boot. Then he looked up, sensing attention from another. The corner of his mouth lifted in an amused grin and he pushed away from the lamppost, heading toward the house. As he passed beneath the boughs of the oak tree, he spared an upward glance. The angel in the tree was most certainly a nice one. Nias allowed a dark smile to cross his lips before he turned away.

The flash of light drew a disquieted sigh from Nichael. The mage truly was fooling with things that would go rapidly beyond his control. As he glanced back down, his gaze narrowed on Nias as the demon passed beneath him.

"You would be better off returning to where you belong."

"And miss all the fun?" Nias shot back over his shoulder. When he reached the house, two massive wings spread out behind him. The moonlight flickered over the black feathers, bringing out their bluish hue. He rose into the air and settled onto the rooftop as his wings lowered. He looked back at Nichael, his smile almost taunting.

Nichael knew who Nias was. His own wings unfurled as he dropped from the tree. With a powerful upward surge, he landed a short distance from Nias. "You aren't here for the fun, so why are you here?"

A deep chuckle resonated in the air between them. "Oh, but tearing a mortal to shreds is fun indeed," Nias purred as his dark gaze slid over Nichael. "Or you could have the puny man inside, and I will ply my trade on you."

"You will be doing neither." Nichael spread his wings to their full length before tucking them against his back. "The man inside is none of your business."

One dark eyebrow rose at that. "And who is going to stop me, oh 'light one'? You?" Nias let out a short laugh and edged along the top of the roof, seeming to take his own sweet time in getting to the other side.

"At this point, I don't think I have to stop you at all," Nichael said.

When Nias disappeared off the roof, his laughter danced in the air around Nichael. Down below on the ground, Nias crept closer to a darkened window from which the bursts of light emanated. He could see nothing but the faintest outline of a figure. Then another flash lit up the room and Nias' eyes widened slightly. He'd expected to see a single man, possibly young, playing with fire, so to speak. What he had not expected was to see a room full of people...and an older-looking mage. He started to rethink his plan of going about this alone.

Paying no more attention to Nias, Nichael created a pocket of energy around himself. Its cell structure began to blend with the energy field of the house as he sank downward. It left no trace of any disturbance to alert the mage of an intruder. He needed to get inside the house to investigate.

Grumbling, Nias dissolved into shadows and seeped into the ground. He emerged inside the house, in a darkened hallway. He could hear the chanting coming from down the hall, but before he could start toward the door, a familiar presence caught hold of his senses.

"Persistent, aren't you, Nichael?"

An annoyed growl sounded from not too far away before Nichael came into view. He fell silent and stiffened before inching toward the door. A painful sensation began to burn him the closer he got to the door.

Nias rolled his eyes and shook his head. "It won't get any better."

No sooner had the words left Nias' mouth than another brilliant flash lit up the room behind the door. Inside the house, the walls and doors shook violently and a deep growl echoed from the room.

"That...was not me," Nias muttered.

Nichael expanded his sight to see beyond the walls and door. He caught the barest glimpse of the light within before he was completely blinded. Staggering back, he clawed at his eyes. He knew the power's source like no other.

Nias caught Nichael before the angel could fall and alert everyone of their presence. When he realized his arms were wrapped around Nichael's waist, he pushed the angel away. "Now that didn't look fucking pleasant. What the hell did you see?"

Nichael didn't look at Nias or even indicate he could no longer see. He reached out for the wall, and stared at what he hoped was the door. "I had only thought..." Trailing off, he shook his head. "He's already tapped into the very source of all of our power. He's twisted it."

"What?" Nias turned the angel around and was startled to see the once-silver eyes were now milky-white. "No fucking way. We need to rethink our plans."

Nichael reached out again, trying to grab hold of the demon. Being more sensitive to the power emanating from the room, he winced when its painful effects scorched through his body. "Get out of here now, Nias."

"Not without you. Gonna need help with this one." Nias growled and picked Nichael up, keeping a tight hold on him as shadows dissolved them both.

The warm sense of energy soothed over the searing pain, and Nichael closed his eyes. He couldn't see Nias, but he could feel him. The demon had managed to surprise the hell out of him.

Nias let out an annoyed growl. This mission was already going to Hell, quite literally, it seemed. He stepped out of the shadows still cradling the blind angel and retreated farther into the cave. There he placed Nichael gently on the smooth stone floor.

"Now, what the hell did you see?"

Nichael needed a moment to regain his bearings while his sight returned. "The mage has managed to create a tear in the inner works of creation. The power... He's accessed it. Just for that short time. That's what I saw." Bemused, Nichael tried to think of how to stop the mage. He'd been seriously caught off guard and didn't plan to be again. "How is it that you were even anywhere near this, Nias?"

Nias' brow wrinkled. "My master sent me to destroy the mage. Why?"

Nichael knew Nias was too young to be anywhere near this. He opened his mouth to say something then closed it. Why Lucifer would want one of his own creatures destroyed was beyond him. Finally he said, "I had thought you were drawn into this out of curiosity."

"No. I managed to piss off the Big Guy by questioning an order. Next thing I know, I'm on a special mission." Nias shrugged. "Guess it keeps me out of his hair for a bit, eh?" he asked, throwing Nichael a wry grin. "Now, how are we going to deal with this mage?"

"Nias, in your case, it might have meant to be permanently out of his hair. How am *I* going to deal with the mage? Very carefully."

Nias narrowed his gaze. "Okay, two things. First, what do you mean by 'permanently'? And second, I do believe you mean 'we'."

Nichael really didn't feel up to spelling it out, but he tried anyway. "The only thing protecting you from what happened in the house was me. I absorbed the waves of power. If you had walked into it by yourself, you would have been destroyed. Very permanently destroyed. Not even your master could handle the power. And that is precisely why I mean I, and not we."

Nias huffed and crossed his arms over his chest. "I was sent to destroy this guy," he said. "I'm not going to back down now. I've been trailing him for some time, but never got close enough until now."

"Did you understand anything I just said?" Nichael shot the demon an annoyed look.

Nias rolled his eyes and stood. "For the most part, yes." He traced his fingers over faded drawings left by the ancient occupants of the cave. "You're welcome, by the way," he said dryly.

"You're just not understanding the important parts." Eyeing him with an arched brow, Nichael asked, "Welcome for what?"

"For getting you out of there. I got us both out before anything else could happen. Instead of getting a 'thank you', I'm getting a fucking lecture."

"I'm supposed to thank you for being smart enough to figure you needed my help?"

Nias opened his mouth, but snapped it shut again. "Whatever," he grumbled. "We still haven't figured out what we're going to do. And I'm still not quite clear on the whole 'permanently destroyed' bit. Why would my master do that?"

"You weren't motivated as I was, Nias. But I can say thank you anyway. As for your master, I'm going to hazard a guess and say he seriously disliked being questioned."

With a dejected sigh, Nias turned and slid down the wall to the cold stone floor. "Well, if Master's intent was to do away with me completely then I guess I'm essentially stuck here."

Nichael frowned. He hated to get involved with this one. It wasn't his place to comfort a demon over losing his position in Hell. The irony was too undeniable. However, he did sense how utterly lost Nias felt. Getting up, he walked toward him and crouched in front of the demon. "You could always prove him wrong, Nias."

"How? If he wants me gone then I'm gone. It's obvious I'm not wanted."

As young as Nias was, Nichael understood the implications of what Lucifer had done. "By helping me. But you have to promise to listen to me. The power the mage is playing with can destroy even me if enough of it is unleashed."

Nias nodded. "I promise. Just be forewarned that I can be brash at times."

"You can't afford it right now because it could get us both destroyed. I could use the help. And I am very thankful you pulled me out of there."

For a brief moment, a smile settled on Nias' lips. He nodded. "I know, and I promise I'll try not to be."

Before Nichael could think better of it, his smile answered the demon's. "Now we need a better place to plan out what has to be done."

The signature of the angel's power surrounded both of them, and in the blink of an eye they were situated in the small house he'd been using for his time here.

Nias blinked rapidly with the sudden change in scenery. "Shit. Warn me next time, will ya?" He stood and stretched his arms over his head. A few seconds later, his wings unfurled to flex the muscles within them. He took care not to disturb anything.

"I thought you'd be more comfortable here. Sorry."

The house was small and sparsely furnished since Nichael didn't require much. Nichael took a moment to study the demon. That Nias was very young was obvious. Twice Nichael had gone out of his way to help him. Yes, it was in his nature, but that didn't account for the twinges he reacted to without thought.

"S'okay," Nias muttered as he looked around. "This your place? Not bad. I never could understand mortals and their need for junk. Give me cigarettes, whiskey and the occasional male body, and I'm happy." He walked over and fingered the cream-colored drapes over the window. His wings fluttered for a minute then settled. "It's been a while since I've been inside a house," he said absently. "Well, other than the mage's."

"Travel light, do you?" Nichael's gaze followed him. Without a doubt, Nias was extremely attractive; Nichael just tried to ignore it. The demon's wavy auburn hair contrasted beautifully with the black feathers of his wings. Apparently Nias preferred modern-day clothing as opposed to the white tunic and pants favored by Nichael. "It serves its purpose while I'm here in this area."

Nias shrugged. "I usually stay in the cave. I have a few connections who supply me with cigarettes and alcohol in exchange for carnal pleasures." He turned and flashed a wicked grin at Nichael. "I get the best of the whole deal, wouldn't you say?"

Raising a brow, Nichael regarded Nias mildly. "I would assume there is more to existence than cigarettes, alcohol and sex. But then I wouldn't be the one qualified to judge whether you are getting the best or not."

"Hey, can't complain when you're shooting your load up some guy's ass while swallowing another cock down your throat." Nias flicked his tongue and licked his lips before he bent over to pick up a book off the top of a nearby stack.

"You must be easily amused. And you mention nothing of emotion. Why is that?"

"Why should I?" Nias mumbled as he flipped through the book. "I've never received any gesture of emotion, so why should I bother opening up?"

"Sometimes it takes the risk of opening up to receive, Nias." While he viewed things dispassionately for the most part, Nichael still understood the give and take required within a meaningful relationship. He approached the demon slowly, looking down at the book in Nias' hand then at him.

"I did," Nias said quietly. "And then I find that my Father has betrayed me. To my connections, I'm nothing more than a body with a cock. There is nothing but physical sensations."

Nichael knew Nias wasn't old enough to be completely corrupt, nor was he influenced by the Fall itself. He also had the feeling Nias didn't understand what could affect one who had suffered through the Fall.

Sighing quietly, he laid his hand on Nias' shoulder. "Lucifer is driven by many things, Nias, and you can't gauge all by what happened. There is more meaning to you than just a body with a cock."

Nias tossed the book onto the floor and pulled away, settling into the armchair a few feet away. "It was merely stupidity on my part," he said bitterly. "Stupidity for thinking I was favored, and stupidity for longing for something I'll never feel with anyone."

"Not stupid, Nias. You wanted something most long for. And something you had a right to expect from him."

Nichael had never doubted the depth of love Michael held for him, but still he understood the impact it would have to have something trusted taken away. He wasn't sure of his ability to reason with Nias, though. Somehow Nichael felt he was floundering over his head.

Nias' head fell back and he closed his eyes. "Yeah, well. Not a fucking chance I'll ever let it happen again. Best to be cold and alone than to have what little heart you have ripped out at the seams."

"That isn't the way to take what happened." Nichael settled heavily into the other chair. It saddened him to listen to Nias, and wanting to reach out and help did him little good. It put him at a loss. "But it seems you'll not listen to me. And in truth, I'm not certain I'm offering much good to you."

"You're listening to me," Nias said. He looked over at Nichael. "That's more than anyone else has ever bothered to do."

Outside of his own complacent universe, Nichael thought little of any other existence. Hearing Nias' words made him pause. "It is little enough, Nias. I understand how you would feel. In your place, I would be devastated."

"I hide it well. Don't suppose you have a shower, do you? Slinking around in that house made me feel..." Nias shivered. "I don't know...odd."

Nichael pointed toward the hall. "Second door on the left. There are towels in the small cupboard as well."

Nichael didn't say anything, but he wasn't surprised by Nias' "feeling odd" comment.

Giving him a nod of thanks, Nias stood and walked out of the room.

Chapter Two

Nias towel-dried his hair before putting his jeans back on. He left his boots and shirt beside the bathroom door, opting for the warm air of the house on his bare skin. His hair was thoroughly disheveled as he walked into the kitchen.

Nichael was busy at the counter. A couple of bags of different chips were opened, and he had a bowl filled with a mixture of them. The rather unnatural addiction to them was the first thing Nias noticed about the angel.

"Feeling better?" Michael asked.

Nias straddled one of the bar stools, hooking his feet on the sides. "Much. Thanks," he said with an amused grin. "At least I'm not the only one who's managed to pick up a few mortal likes along the way."

"I believe cigarettes and alcohol are mortal habits. At least mine are less hazardous." Smirking slightly at Nias, Nichael leaned comfortably against the counter and ate a handful of chips.

"Hazardous to mortals," Nias said. "Not to me. Besides, alcohol has a distinct burn, almost like a man's come. It's addictive."

"You seem to have a one-track mind. I certainly hope you don't plan on bringing anybody here for your own amusement."

"No worries," Nias said, seconds before he grinned wolfishly. "Besides, the eye candy is enough."

"I'm not here for your amusement either." Nichael's tone was dry.

"You ruffle easily." Nias chuckled.

Nichael fell silent, eating some of his chips. His gaze never left Nias', the silvery depths glittering faintly with his own amusement.

Nias slid off of the stool and bent over the counter, reaching into the bowl for a chip. "Stupid question, but where do you want me to sleep? I only saw one bedroom."

"You can have the couch. It's comfortable enough."

Nias turned and walked to the couch. He stretched out on it, resting his arms under his head. One foot hung off of the edge, while the other was drawn up. Even from the distance, he could see the angel clearly and he let his gaze wander over Nichael's body for the first time since meeting him. Oh, yeah, the angel definitely looked good.

Nichael caught the inviting look Nias gave him. Ignoring the stirring he felt at the idea, Nichael said, "If I thought you would behave, you could share my bed." He closed up the bags and put them back in the cupboard.

"I couldn't promise that," Nias said quietly.

"Then it would be better if you slept on the couch."

"And such a lonely, cold bed it will be."

"Somehow I doubt you would appreciate the fact that I prefer it that way," Nichael said. "It leaves more room for me."

"Suit yourself," Nias said with a shrug. "Body heat does wonders. Aren't you going to sit down?"

Carefully, Nichael sat at the open end of the couch. He wasn't all that happy to be aware of the demon. Nias' presence nagged at the fringes of Nichael's mind, reminding him of how close they were. Several choice words were already forming in his thoughts, and he planned to express them to Michael as soon as he could.

"Don't you have any other thoughts to occupy you, Nias?"

"Like...?" Nias prodded. One hand rubbed absently over his chest and stomach.

"Anything that doesn't include sexual gratification?"

Nias' expression didn't change as his fingers brushed over the crease of his hip before settling on the inside of his upper thigh. "Are you saying there's something wrong with it?"

Nichael knew he was being played, but even knowing it, he reacted. Abruptly he stood. "If you don't think there is, apparently there isn't." Without a backward glance, Nichael went down the hall to his bedroom.

It had been some time since Nichael had been home.

The atmosphere relaxed him as he soaked in the heavier presence permeating the halls. He sighed in contentment as he strode into the throne room.

Looking up, the man on the throne smiled. With a wave of his hand, the others departed, leaving the two of them alone. He rose and his emerald wings stretched out then dropped back down. He motioned toward one of the corners where white and gold pillows waited.

"What brings you home?" Michael asked as he settled down, leaning back against the wall with a smug look on his face.

Nichael bowed his head to Michael. Normally he didn't bother his prince with details. Nichael tended to handle his missions with uncanny success. It bothered him to no end to be disturbing Michael now, but he didn't feel he had a choice. "I have encountered an unexpected problem, Michael."

"Oh? And that would be?"

"A young demon, a very young demon." Nichael wasn't used to the emotional roller coaster of one minute wanting to help Nias, and the next wanting to strangle him. "I've taken him in, but I can't have him around while I try to deal with the mage. Nias is likely to get himself killed."

"Ah, yes," Michael said. "Nias. He must be quite the handful if he already has you twisted into such knots."

"Could you please find a place for him, Michael?"

"I already have, Nichael, and he seems to be doing quite well."

"You don't mean me. I'm not sure if I can really help

him. I've tried, but I don't think I'm doing much good."

Michael stood and placed his hands on Nichael's shoulders. He pressed a soft kiss to Nichael's forehead and whispered, "He isn't the one who needs it, my friend."

The words only served to confuse Nichael further, but then when it came to Nias that particular emotion was commonplace.

"Look at me, Nichael. You need each other. You have a great deal in common, if only you open your eyes and heart to see it."

Nichael wanted to argue, but it would do him no good. "I will do my best with him, Michael." *If I don't kill him first.*

"Open your heart to him, and try not to kill each other."

"I think you have more faith in me than I do."

"My faith is unerring. Take care of him. He needs you, Nichael, just as you need him."

"I will do as you ask, and fulfill my duty."

Nichael wasn't sure how he would manage, but he would do his best as he always did. After bowing his head once again to Michael, he entered the portal near him. Nichael wasn't fully sure what to make of everything Michael had said. When he stepped into his living room, he was no less confused than he had been earlier.

Nias lay fast asleep, stretched out on the couch, one hand low on his bare stomach, his fingers fanned. Nichael realized just how young Nias was, no matter what the demon portrayed when he was awake. Nichael crouched beside the couch.

Nias stretched in his sleep, the movement tightening his muscles then relaxing them. His eyes opened. He turned his head to look at Nichael. "Welcome home."

Odd how Nichael's own expression softened when his gaze met Nias'. Even odder was the feeling descending over him. "I didn't mean to wake you."

"S'okay," Nias said sleepily. "I think I could get used to it if given the chance."

Unable to resist the urge, Nichael reached out and brushed back Nias' hair from his forehead. "We'll be stuck together for a while, so you'll probably have to get used to it."

As Nias closed his eyes, a sound greatly resembling a purr rumbled from his throat. With a lightning fast move, he had Nichael's hand in his. He pressed a kiss to each fingertip then opened his mouth, sucking two into velvet heat. Nichael hissed. Even knowing he should draw back his hand, he didn't.

Nias began sucking, rolling his tongue around Nichael's fingers with every pull. Swallowing thickly, Nichael tried to control the effect Nias had on him. He finally managed to pull back his hand.

"I'm not a thing for you to play with, Nias."

For the briefest moment, a look of hurt passed through the demon's eyes. He shook his head and sat up. "I need a shower," he said as he stood. He started down the hall, his shoulders a bit lower than normal.

The demon tended to be a very sexual creature, Nichael hadn't missed that. Nor had he missed the pained expression. Straightening, he watched Nias uncertainly. He followed behind him, laying a hand on Nias' shoulder before he entered the bathroom. "Was I wrong?"

Nias sighed and hung his head. "Wrong about what?" he said without looking up. He leaned forward, pressing his forehead to the doorframe. "I just..." With another sigh, he shook his head. "Never mind."

"I hurt you, and that wasn't my intention." Nichael exerted a gentle pressure to Nias' shoulder to get him to turn around and look at him. "You just what?"

"I just thought... I swore not to trust anyone ever again, but for some reason, it just comes naturally with you. Whether I really want to or not." Nias laughed. "And I can't exactly deny that I'm attracted to you. I guess I was just hoping it was mutual. Believe it or not, I won't do anything against a man's will."

It wasn't hard for Nichael to see the beauty shining within Nias. "Perhaps not so odd. I am attracted to you as well." He wasn't certain they had a place together, no matter what Michael had told him. Though he'd gotten the feeling Michael might be playing matchmaker. "You are very beautiful, Nias. More beautiful than anyone I have seen in a long time."

Nias opened his mouth then shut it just as quickly. He looked away as his cheeks flushed pink. "That's a first."

"I think it may be why everything happened to you,

Nias." Nichael smoothed a fingertip over the demon's skin.

Nias turned his face into Nichael's touch. "I wouldn't be surprised. I'm sorry if I assumed anything with you."

"I owe you an apology as well," Nichael said. "For my own assumption. Go ahead and take your shower. I'll be waiting in the living room."

Nias swallowed hard and nodded, closing the door between them.

Lost in thought, Nichael returned to the living room. Any relationship between them would be impossible. It wasn't something he wanted. He preferred his well-ordered life as it was. Those thoughts warred with something deeper inside him.

Twenty minutes later, Nias returned, drying his hair with his towel. He leaned up against the counter. After a few minutes of silence, he spoke. "Look, I really am sorry. I didn't mean to make you uncomfortable."

"You haven't made me uncomfortable. Annoyed me occasionally, but not made me uncomfortable, Nias. I'm just not used to any disruptions to my duty."

"I'm not sure if I should take that as a compliment or not." Chuckling, Nias turned and bent over the counter, reaching for the bowl of chips he'd filled earlier.

"At least you're not taking offense."

"No. I'm not offended," Nias said with a mouthful of potato chips. He picked up the bowl and walked over to the couch, dropping beside Nichael and offering him a chip. "Humor me," he whispered as he touched the chip to Nichael's lips.

"As long as you humor me."

"Anything you want."

"Why do I get the feeling you're saying a lot more beneath the surface?"

"What do you wish of me?"

"I don't know. What do you want of me?"

"A kiss," Nias said.

To grant that would be easy enough on the surface, but Nichael knew how much it might cost him. Once started, he wasn't certain one kiss would be enough. He drew the demon toward him. Nias traced his tongue over Nichael's lips then probed between them, seeking entrance. His fingers tangled in Nichael's hair, holding him close.

Something between a purr and a growl slipped from Nias as he deepened the kiss. His tongue swept through Nichael's mouth, circling Nichael's tongue. His fingers tightened in Nichael's hair as the sound grew stronger. Then he pulled away, breathless and dazed. "I can't," he said, shaking his head. "If I don't stop, I'm going to want more."

Nichael already found himself lost in something he barely understood. The kiss had proved intoxicating, and his first reaction was to blurt out not to stop. Biting his lower lip, he stifled the plea.

Nias leaned over and ran his fingers through his hair. "I want you," he growled. "I want you so fucking bad it's eating away at me. But I said one kiss and I stand by my word."

"We need to take care of other things, Nias." Nichael stood abruptly and paced in front of the couch. He needed to focus on his duty, on what he was supposed to be doing.

Within seconds, Nias bolted off of the couch and shoved him against the wall, pinning him tightly as he crushed his mouth to Nichael's. He forced his tongue into the angel's mouth and gripped Nichael's wrists, holding them in an iron grip.

Sensations shot straight through Nichael and he instantly hardened in response. Part of him understood the need taking hold of Nias because it drenched him as well. He arched toward Nias, forgetting everything he'd been trying to think of.

"You think too much," Nias growled into Nichael's mouth. "And there are other things to do with that beautiful mouth besides talking." Locking both of Nichael's wrists in one hand, Nias slid his other hand between them, gripping Nichael through his pants. "You need to feel."

The need for another wasn't something normally dominating the angel's thoughts, but now his thoughts were scattered. His hips nudged into the press of Nias' hand as he groaned. All he wanted to do was touch. "Then let me feel more."

Nias slipped his hand inside Nichael's pants, wrapping his fingers tightly around the angel's cock. He began stroking it, milking his hand up and down the shaft. "What do you want to feel, Nichael? My hands? My mouth? My ass? My cock?" He kissed a slow path over Nichael's cheek to his ear, flicking his tongue across it. "Or everything?"

"Everything." The silky pressure of Nias' hand on his cock drew a slow shudder from Nichael. It had been too long since he'd allow another to touch him. Freeing his hands from Nias' grip, he slid them up into Nias' hair. Turning his head, he caught the demon's lips, the hungry probe of his tongue parting them for a deeper kiss.

"Don't move," Nias murmured.

He kissed his way down Nichael's throat, his chest, his stomach. He knelt down, tugging Nichael's pants to his feet. He wasted no time and wrapped his fingers around Nichael's cock once more as he leaned forward. He rolled his eyes up to hold Nichael's gaze as his tongue snaked out and circled the head of his cock, teasing at the slit. Then he sucked on the tip.

Chapter Three

Nichael leaned against the wall, seriously needing the support. Another shudder ran through him, and he couldn't control the sudden thrust of his hips. Nias purred, the vibrations rippling through Nichael's cock. He gripped Nichael's hips in his hands and began sliding his mouth up and down his shaft, stopping to suck on the tip before swallowing him once more. He stroked the underside with his tongue, humming softly with every stroke. He looked up again, locking a hungry gaze on Nichael.

"Get up, Nias, and go over to the couch." Nichael pulled the demon to his feet. Nias swallowed hard, the hunger sharp in his eyes. He backed up to the couch and fell onto it.

After stepping out of his pants and shoes, Nichael began to remove his tunic. He smiled at the feast spread before him. Once he was near the couch, he reached down to unfasten Nias' pants. He couldn't deny his need, the insatiable urge to take Nias as his own.

Nias lifted his hips, allowing Nichael to pull off his jeans. He swept his gaze over Nichael, the look in his eyes hungry. Nichael's actions remained unhurried as he tugged off the jeans and dropped them to the floor. His fingers drifted over Nias' chest, the demon irresistible. Without a word, Nichael knelt beside the couch.

He was in no hurry to take what he wanted. He savored the sight of the body stretched out just for him. From Nias' expression, Nichael knew how much the demon wanted him. Leaning forward slightly, Nichael kissed Nias' chest and lightly scraped his teeth over Nias' nipple before he drew it into his mouth. He traced a path down Nias' stomach to circle his navel.

Nias drew in a sharp breath, threading his fingers in Nichael's hair. He shivered under Nichael's touch, muscles flexing, moving beneath Nichael's lips and fingers. Without a doubt, Nichael knew that Nias' skin would prove to be an addiction all its own. He took his time, holding Nias' nipple captive in his mouth as he flicked the tip of his tongue back and forth against it. "What do you want to feel, Nias?" Nichael whispered, lips barely brushing Nias' chest.

"You. Everything." Nias found Nichael's other hand and pulled it to his mouth. "Your touch, your taste." He rolled his tongue around two of Nichael's fingers then sucked them into his mouth. His other hand moved down to brush over Nichael's, entwining their fingers around his own cock. His breath caught as he stroked their joined hands over his length. "I need..." His hips lifted and a soft whimper escaped him. "I need to feel you inside me, Nichael."

Seeing the open vulnerability on Nias' features,

111

Nichael felt it tug at something inside him. More than lust drove him. His expression softened as he stared into the black eyes. Nichael understood in a moment of perfect clarity that Nias needed far more than that.

"I want my own taste first, Nias." After releasing Nias' cock, Nichael lifted him until the demon was exposed to him. Nichael lowered his head and rimmed Nias' hole with his tongue.

"Nichael. Please..." Nichael licked the puckered skin and resumed stroking the demon's cock. When he breached Nias' body, however, he was greeted by an unexpected tightness and it gave him a moment's pause. He definitely hadn't expected that. Nichael studied Nias for a silent moment before he changed position. He settled over the demon, and for a moment, he savored the feel of the body beneath him. A sharp ache had already taken up residence in Nichael, and nothing would stop him from taking everything Nias offered.

Nias threaded his hands through Nichael's hair, pulling him down for a kiss. He spread his legs farther apart, moaning into Nichael's mouth as their cocks slid together. His kiss was hungry, yet nervous. "I need this, Nichael," he whispered, breaking the kiss. "I need you."

Nichael lowered his head and nuzzled Nias' throat. "As much as I need you."

"Nichael, please..." Nias pleaded softly, arching his body toward Nichael's. "Inside me. I need you inside me. I know it will hurt. I can handle the pain."

"Soon, Nias." Quickly wetting his hand, Nichael

stroked over his own cock before rubbing the head over Nias' entrance. He kissed Nias softly then thrust.

Nias cried out and his fingers dug into Nichael's hips, holding him still. "Don't move," he breathed. "Oh..." His chest rose and fell quickly, his black gaze locking onto Nichael's.

The sensation enveloping his cock tore away at Nichael's self-control. He managed to calm himself somewhat only by focusing on the soft caress of his hands over Nias' hips. "You have no idea of how beautiful you are, Nias."

"I don't know what's in my soul," Nias said. A look of confusion crossed his face. "But whatever is there...is yours."

"And I want everything of you as my own." Nichael tucked his wings around both of them. This was meant only for him—for them. A gentle rock of his hips kept him buried within the demon. The touch of his lips molded to Nias' before his tongue sought entry into the demon's mouth. His movements were unhurried as he withdrew slightly only to fill Nias again as he made love to him. Soon it would be more, but he wanted Nias to feel something other than lust for once.

Meeting Nichael with a rock of his hips, Nias cried out, the sound drowned in their kiss. He shook beneath Nichael, fingers smoothing over Nichael's wings. The touch set off a chain reaction in Nichael. He sped up, panting into the demon's mouth. A determined push of his hips strained toward Nias' body with a violent shudder as Nichael's orgasm swept through him. Breaking away from the kiss, he shouted. Lightning flooding his body with pleasure.

"Nichael!" Nias went still for a split second then he bucked, driving Nichael deeper. Between them, his cock throbbed, spilling his release. It took several minutes for him to stop shaking and he squeezed his eyes shut, struggling to catch his breath.

"Never felt anything like that," Nias said once he'd caught his breath. "Never knew something could feel like that."

Carefully Nichael withdrew and lay down. He pulled Nias onto his side, the demon pinned to the back of the couch. Nichael kept his left wing tucked around Nias to shelter him. "It's going to feel like that many times between us, Nias."

"You were the first," Nias said. He looked up at Nichael. "And you will be the only one. I was serious when I said everything I have is yours."

It meant a great deal to Nichael that Nias had been willing to give him that. He smoothed his fingers over the dark hair as he studied his lover in turn. "I wouldn't be willing to share you with anyone. Not now and not ever. And you have the same from me in return."

"What is this? I don't understand any of this. Desire and lust, I understand. But this?" Nias shook his head. "There is more than just desire and lust."

"It is a lot more than that, Nias. I am incapable of feeling only lust."

Nias smiled and scooted closer. His tongue slid along Nichael's lips then slipped inside. Relaxed, he draped his arms around Nichael's neck.

Opening fully to the demon, Nichael encouraged the exploration with soft flicks of his tongue. He knew Nias didn't truly understand, but the demon would in time. And during that time, Nichael would keep his lover protected and very well loved.

℃℈

This was stupid. Stupid, stupid, stupid. What was he thinking? Nias knew he was in trouble as the man watched him. Nias fully believed he wouldn't get caught, that he could scout things out by himself, prove that he was strong. He'd left Nichael asleep in the apartment and wanted to prove himself, to show that he was strong enough. He'd been mistaken, and that mistake might very well have sealed his fate.

"Aren't you an interesting catch?"

Nias tugged on the chains holding him, but found they had no give. He wanted to reach out and strangle the godforsaken life out of the damned mage, but he couldn't even move more than half an inch from the wall. Adding insult to injury, the chains were enchanted, preventing him from being anything more than flesh and blood. And judging by the dark look in the mage's eyes, Nias had a feeling he wouldn't even be that for much longer.

"You have no idea what you are messing with," Nias

growled. "You are playing with fire."

"And you have no way to stop me. There is real fear in your eyes. You are mine now, in service to only me. And I will see to it once your service to me is finished, you are destroyed."

ᨆ

It took no more than overwhelming fear to pull Nichael to Nias' location like a magnet. He stood outside the mage's house in a rage. Using only a minor expenditure of energy, he merged with the magic protecting the house, remaining invisible as he walked down the corridor to the room where he could feel the disrupting vibration. Passing through the door, he emerged on the other side just in time to hear the mage's pronouncement.

Brilliant light surrounded Nias' body, rendering the chains useless as they fell away from him. The mage, blinded by brightness, never saw the backhanded blow from Nichael that sent him crashing into the wall.

As the mage screamed in pain and rage, Nias grabbed Nichael's hand. The mage stumbled to his feet, still blind and dazed, and reached out in Nias' direction. "You are mine!" the man screamed.

An enraged snarl answered the mage and Nichael's white wings stretched out in an aggressive stance. Only Nias' pull on him focused Nichael's attention back on the demon, and his power surrounded them both. One moment they were in the mage's hall, the next they were safely in their own living room. Nichael tugged Nias against him.

"Before you say anything, I know that was stupid," Nias said, his voice muffled.

"What possessed you to do that, Nias?" Nichael tried to rein in his sudden burst of temper, and it was proving almost too difficult for him. The idea of the mage imprisoning Nias and the last words he'd screamed at them were doing a number on Nichael.

Nias sighed, but didn't move. "I wanted to spy on him, try to find out what he's up to and how to stop him. I didn't want you to... I didn't want you to get hurt." He burrowed his face in the fall of hair covering Nichael's neck and shoulder, and whispered, "I love you too much to lose you."

Tightening his hold around Nias, Nichael drew the demon with him toward the couch. As he sat, he pulled Nias onto his lap. Surprised warred with his own initial reaction; Nichael hadn't thought Nias would admit to what he felt. Pulling his head back, he stared steadily at him. "And I love you too much to lose you, Nias. I will protect you with my life if need be." No way would Nichael ever let that mage get his hands on Nias again. He'd kill the bastard first.

"I'm sorry," Nias whispered. "I won't let you go alone, and I'm no match for him. We're going to have to work together. I know that, whether I like it or not."

"I don't want you anywhere near him again." The

anger settled back into his expression as Nichael scowled. He could and would take care of the mage. He'd already gotten a bit of information on his own, and had set things up for the mage to come looking for him.

Nias glared at Nichael. "I will not sit idly by and watch him try to destroy you. We're in this together."

"And I will not let him enslave and destroy you, Nias," Nichael countered vehemently. "You are mine, not his. You will never be his."

Nias opened his mouth to argue further, but then seemed to think better of it. "I'm not going to win this one, am I?"

"No, not on this." With a gentle touch, Nichael brushed back the ebony hair from Nias' cheek. "I can protect myself from him. Even if he thought to destroy me, he wouldn't succeed permanently. I would return."

Nias closed his eyes and sighed. "I don't think that's something I could ever survive watching, Nichael."

Nichael gently ran his fingertips beneath Nias' chin, drawing the demon's face up to look at him again. "For my sake, don't say that, Nias. What would I have to return to if you weren't here for me?"

Meeting his gaze, Nias smiled. "I don't belong in this realm any more than you do, but I will always be wherever you need me." He leaned forward and kissed Nichael softly. "Besides, I'd miss your stubbornness."

Gazing steadily at him for a long moment, Nichael said nothing. He wanted Nias constantly at his side. Once the mage was taken care of, he would see to it. "You belong with me, always with me."

⊗

Nias knew the second he woke up that something was wrong—he was alone. He threw off the blankets and, not giving a damn that he was naked, wandered out of the bedroom, expecting to see Nichael making coffee or engaged in some other bizarre human habit. But when he realized Nichael was gone, he started to panic.

The first place he thought to look was the mage's house. After he dressed, that was exactly where he went, keeping out of sight as he watched the house closely for any sign of his angel.

Suddenly the angel appeared out of the blue, hovering over the house. From the state he was in, it was clear he'd been in a battle. A portion of his body had been burned, and the white of his wings showed many burn areas as well. A scowl marred Nichael's fair features and the sword in his hand was covered in blood.

Nias' eyes widened. When he was finally able to move, he spread his wings and flew to Nichael, hovering beside him. Common sense aside, he started looking the angel over frantically.

"What happened? You're hurt! Shit!"

Sheathing the sword, Nichael scanned the area to make sure they were safe. "I'm all right, Nias. Just a little the worse for wear."

"Fuck," Nias hissed, reaching out to brush his fingers over singed feathers. "What the fuck happened?"

Even with the light touch, Nichael winced. "I took care of some of the mage's comrades, but the little bastard escaped me. I was sure he would return to the house, but I can't sense him anywhere around here."

"C'mon," Nias urged, tugging at Nichael's arm. "Home. We'll find him later. You need to heal."

If Nichael hadn't felt so weary, he probably wouldn't have agreed to leave. As it was, he nodded to Nias and moved closer to him, drawing the demon under his mantle of power. In no more than a blink, they were standing in their living room. "I think I could use a long, hot bath and a night next to you."

Nias was already undressing him, pushing Nichael's shirt off his shoulders as he leaned in for a kiss. "Need you. Need to know you're okay."

Thankfully, Nichael wasn't in as much pain as he'd been before Nias saw him. Smiling slowly, Nichael leaned toward Nias, resting his hand on his lover's shoulder. A soft brush of his lips touched the demon's cheek. "I'm an angel, remember? I'll heal."

"Don't care," Nias grumbled, almost growled, fingers working on Nichael's pants. "Want to see, want to touch. Fuck. You're mine to touch, not theirs."

There was no scarring on Nichael's body from the burns since they'd already healed. Only the blackened marks remained, but some of the material of his clothes had been burned into his skin. Nor had he bothered fixing the serious singeing to his wings.

"You're allowed that, Nias." Nichael let Nias have his way. Very carefully he began peeling the material of the shirt away from his skin. It stuck in places, and he had to tug to get it off.

Nias' growls were growing stronger as every inch of Nichael's body was revealed. "They touched you," he snarled, tossing strips of the tattered shirt to the floor. "They hurt you." He shoved Nichael's pants to the floor.

Realizing nothing he said would calm the demon, Nichael let Nias rant. He realized what Nias would need to do and expended a portion of energy to heal the torn skin and blackened feathers. After stepping out of the pants, he reached for Nias. He started them slowly backward toward the bathroom, brushing feather-light kisses across Nias' skin.

Nias' hands mapped Nichael's body as if searching. When they reached the bathroom, he shoved Nichael against the doorframe and pushed his tongue into Nichael's mouth, low growls filling the kiss.

Nichael opened to him with no resistance, and Nias' possessive wave of frenetic energy engulfed him. Nichael circled around the demon's neck with his arms, pressing closer to him. Their kiss inflamed his senses and he reacted hungrily to it.

"In the shower. Want to touch and taste and fuck you until the end of time." Nipping at Nichael's lower lip, Nias stepped away and went to the bathtub. He started the water and stripped then reached for Nichael.

Nichael pushed Nias back into the shower. The spray of hot water hit them both as he covered Nias' lips with his own. He explored every inch he could reach, hands caressing and kneading downward over Nias' arms.

Nias gripped Nichael's hips, tugging him, pushing their cocks together. "Need you," he whispered. "Want to taste..." He slid down Nichael's body, taking Nichael's cock into his mouth in one breath.

Leaning heavily against the cool tile of the wall, Nichael groaned. He stared down at the demon, everything forgotten to the one lone sensation of Nias' mouth. Nichael enjoyed it all with slow movements of his hips, sliding his cock in and out between Nias' lips.

Tongue stroking the underside, Nias worked the flesh in his mouth, teeth grazing just the slightest bit. He curled his fingers around Nichael's hips, nails digging into the skin as he encouraged the movements.

Nichael jerked harder and quicker, burying himself in the wet heat. A deeper groan escaped him and before it could go too far, he tugged the demon's hair to draw Nias away. "Not that way, Nias. I want to be inside you."

Licking his lips, Nias looked up from where he knelt, one hand stroking himself slowly. "Please."

Nichael drew Nias up and spun him to face the wall. He bent Nias at the waist and stepped back, reaching to point the spray of water at Nias' ass. He massaged the cheeks of the demon's ass, parting them to the water, enjoying the sight of the tight, beckoning hole waiting for him.

Nias groaned and placed his palms against the tiled wall, spreading his legs. "Yes..." His head dropped down, back arching. "Please, Nichael..."

Nichael dipped his fingers between the cheeks, rubbing slowly against the crack before lowering to circle Nias' anus. Watching Nias intently, he pushed one finger inside, wiggling it and probing deeper. Before Nias could react, Nichael withdrew his finger and replaced it with his cock. With one slow push of his hips, he sank inside. Buried balls-deep, he leaned over and licked the water from Nias' skin.

"Nichael." Nias pushed back impatiently. He shivered, and the sound of nails grating on the white tile warred with the thrum of the water pouring down on them.

Slow, easy movements impaled Nias. Nichael slipped one hand around to cup Nias' balls, gently tugging and playing with them. "Give in to me, Nias."

Nias shook and cried out. Two massive wings fanned out, the water soaking the black feathers. His tail started as a nub and grew, the barb at the tip just barely grazing Nichael's skin as the tail coiled around the angel's waist. "Harder," Nias begged, fingernails lengthening into razor-sharp claws.

Giving him exactly what he asked for, Nichael began to fuck Nias in a hard, fast rhythm, the slap of their flesh overpowering the sound of the water. Gripping Nias' hip, he forced the demon back against the brutal motion. His other hand tightened around Nias' cock, stroking quickly to bring Nias closer to the edge. Nichael bit sharply at the demon's shoulder, his teeth sinking into Nias, drawing blood. The sweetness flooded Nichael and he came, thrusting deep. Nias roared as heat poured over Nichael's fist.

Nichael pulled back and turned Nias around. He drew Nias' face against his throat. For several long moments, he simply held on, humming softly.

"Love." The one word was breathed across Nichael's skin. Nias followed it with soft kisses. "Mine."

In answer, Nichael completely opened himself, the ephemeral energy joining them into one mind. In that, he gave everything of himself to the demon and nothing was withheld. In return, Nichael accepted everything Nias was and all the demon gave to him. Words weren't necessary. They both understood now.

ORDER OF THE HIGHEST

Chapter One

Sprawled in the booth, Talah ignored the others around him. Most were far older and more seasoned than he was. The main headquarters of the Damnation subsect of the Faction of the Disillusioned was no more than a rundown dive of a bar in the worst part of the fourth planet of the universe. An area overrun by the Disillusioned.

While Talah might be young, he wasn't stupid by any means. He avoided the notice of the others simply by ignoring them. As long as he stayed out of their way, there'd be no problem. Most of the conversations around him were low-voiced, and Talah made no attempt to listen in.

With a grunt, an angel settled across from him. The taint covering him nearly made Talah bolt out of the seat. Normally most fallen were extremely proficient at hiding their status. The only thing that revealed them to Talah was their presence here. This one seemed to take pride in the taint surrounding him. "I was told you're looking for a new Order. The White Light not enough for the likes of you?"

Talah smirked. "No."

"The name's Oriyas. Ever hear of the Order of the Highest?"

Nodding, Talah waited for further explanation. The Highest were far more powerful and organized than the Order of White Light. After he'd nearly become a pawn in the internal backstabbing prevalent in the White Light, Talah had sought out the Disillusioned as a far better ideal to be aligned with.

"Leave the White Light and go there," Oriyas said.

When Oriyas didn't continue, Talah stared at him. Angels didn't normally leave their own Orders, though it wasn't abnormal to request to be trained by another Order. Given the White Light's growing reputation, Talah probably wouldn't have too much trouble getting away from them. But would a body like the Highest accept him into its Order?

"Is this the new one?" Another angel placed his hand on Talah's shoulder and leaned closer to him with a grin.

"Yeah. Talah, this is Sepha," Oriyas answered. "You'll be reporting to him once you've gotten into the Highest."

"Pretty boy, and young, too." Turning his head, Sepha licked beneath Talah's ear, his breath hot. Sepha's voice lowered to a whisper. "And I taste innocence in you."

Talah did his best to still his own disturbing response.

"Leave him to me, Oriyas. I'll take care of him." Sepha ran his hand down Talah's arm then applied a bruising grip to pull him up. The other angel nodded then stood and abruptly left.

"I think you'll remain with me for a short time before you join the Highest." An implacable note in the voice whispering to him told Talah it wasn't likely he'd be given much of a choice. Talah freed his arm with a jerk then motioned to Sepha to lead the way.

One dark brow rose and Sepha eyed him with a cruel smile. "So much spirit. It will be a pleasure taming it."

Talah ignored the comment and waited until Sepha started for the door. Following behind, Talah kept his thoughts carefully hidden.

It was clear Sepha planned on making use of him. The notion didn't really bother Talah, since he had every intention of doing the same. As he followed Sepha through the dark streets, neither of them said a word. The whole time, Talah remained aware of the nearly overwhelming sense of Sepha's presence surrounding him.

Sepha led the way up a narrow flight of stairs and opened the first door at the top of the landing. Entering behind him, Talah was surprised when he stepped into an enormous, luxuriously decorated room. Huge red draperies hung from two-story windows. Through the open drapes, Talah could see the night sky.

The red, gold and black color scheme fit Sepha. He wore black pants with a red tunic. The material clung to his rugged form, keeping Talah's gaze on the demon. Though Talah hadn't seen Sepha's wings, he had the feeling they would be golden. Probably a darker shade than Sepha's shoulder-length hair. The fallen angel's eyes were gold as well, giving him a rather unsettling but undeniably beautiful, appearance.

"Who are you?" Talah asked.

"You'll find out when I want you to, Talah." Sepha drew Talah up the wide, sweeping staircase. They walked down the narrow hallway at the top. Talah wondered what the hell was going on. Stopping in front of a closed door, Sepha opened it. "This is your room while you are here."

After pulling Talah into the room, Sepha turned to face him. He tightened his hand around Talah's as a darker look crossed Sepha's features. "It is also my room. Is my meaning clear?"

Talah knew Sepha wasn't giving him a choice at all, but it really didn't matter. Talah had no problem going along with it for as long as it fit his own plans. Releasing Sepha's hand, he stepped close enough to Sepha to drape his arms around the demon's neck. "Do I look like I'm going to complain?"

Without giving him a chance to answer, Talah kissed him, tongue pushing between Sepha's lips for a taste. A soft growl answered Talah before Sepha's arms went around his waist and pulled him flush with the hardness of the demon's body.

Talah felt an impatient hand tug at the waistband of his pants then the heat of Sepha's hand gliding over the bare skin of his hip as his pants fell to the floor. Talah stepped out of his pants and, with an equal lack of patience, he started on Sepha's pants, nearly tearing the material.

Sepha laughed before he quickly shed his clothing,

baring a fine, muscled body. Talah's shirt joined Sepha's on the floor then Talah went to his knees in front of the fallen angel. Sepha's cock was long and thick, nestled in gold curls. Talah grasped the base and drew it to his mouth, licking the head. He didn't miss the reactive shudder of Sepha's body and the insistent push of the demon's cock into his mouth. A quick suction engulfed the hard flesh as Talah took Sepha in fully. A low groan rewarded him, and he looked upward to meet Sepha's gaze.

A darker need had replaced the earlier laughter in the gold eyes. Talah could feel its pull on him, yet he refused to give in to it. Sepha grabbed his head, forcing Talah to a quicker pace. Wrapping his mouth fully around Sepha's cock, Talah came close to the base as he relaxed his throat. A sharp cry erupted from Sepha and several shudders rolled through him as he fucked Talah's mouth then filled it with the hot spurts of his come. Talah swallowed the thick liquid, cleaned Sepha's cock then drew back to settle on his feet.

"What a sweet mouth you have." A single talon trailed over Talah's lips. "Now I want to know if your ass is just as sweet."

Saying nothing, Talah stood and headed for the bed. As he positioned himself on his hands and knees, Sepha spent a moment preparing. Talah felt Sepha press against his ass a moment later and, with no warning, Sepha buried himself fully inside.

Ripples of pain accompanied the burning stretch of his ass, but Talah didn't make a sound. Sepha wrapped his fingers in Talah's hair and jerked his head back as the demon's other hand gripped Talah's hips. Talah's own need sharpened and he reached for his cock, the sensations spurred by the sheer brutality. Talah pumped his fist in time with Sepha's thrusts and his body tightened. The pure pain and pleasure assaulted his senses, and finally he gave into them. As he came, he ground tightly back against Sepha.

Before Talah could come down, Sepha's hands held his hips, pinning him in place. Contracting inner muscles, Talah pushed hard against Sepha as the demon filled his ass.

When he finally released Talah, Sepha ran a talon lightly up Talah's back before burying in his hair. A hard tug brought Talah against Sepha's body. "You please me, Talah. It's been too long since I've had anyone as young and sweet as you."

Careful to keep his smile from showing, Talah turned his head, seeking Sepha's kiss.

ॐ

Sepha proved to be a vicious fighter. For the first time, Talah found an opponent worth learning from. Circling Sepha warily, Talah looked for an opening to get beneath the demon's defenses. Sepha turned slowly with him, gold eyes narrowed on Talah.

Talah feinted to the left in an effort to distract his opponent, but Sepha moved in the opposite direction just as Talah rushed him. Drawn up short, Talah abruptly stopped.

Laughing, Sepha took to the air before he quickly dropped back down behind Talah. A strong pair of arms imprisoned Talah from behind and pinned him against the hard line of Sepha's body. "You have much to learn, precious. I'm going to take great pleasure in teaching you."

A hard backward jerk of Talah's head connected with Sepha's chin and the hold instantly loosened on him. Darting away, Talah laughed as he whirled to face Sepha again.

"Very good." Sepha laughed and rubbed his chin. "Lesson done for the day."

Talah relaxed his stance then approached Sepha. Occasionally the fallen angel could be easily distracted by his lust, and Talah didn't hesitate to play to it. As Talah stopped in front of Sepha, the demon reached for him, pulling open Talah's tunic. Then Talah felt the sharpness of Sepha's talons dragging over his chest.

"When am I to go on my mission?" Talah asked as he arched toward Sepha. Sepha had kept him in the house for several weeks already, and Talah had no clue as to when the demon planned on releasing him.

"I will decide that in my own time." The sharp bite of Sepha's teeth at Talah's throat followed his answer.

Sepha wanted his blood and Talah knew it. The demon had a taste for blood and fed almost nightly from Talah as they fucked. Piercing the skin in a hard bite,

Sepha took what he wanted. A sharp burn flooded Talah and the rock of his hips encouraged Sepha. Their cocks rubbed together, restrained only by the thin cloth of their pants.

Talah couldn't deny that the demon aroused a great deal of lust in him, but Sepha thought he controlled far more than he actually did. Talah preferred to let him continue believing that. Feeling the hard pull of Sepha's mouth against his skin, Talah slid his hands beneath Sepha's shirt and kneaded Sepha's skin with his nails.

Insuring Talah constantly felt the lure of power had become Sepha's way of attempting to possess Talah. Talah allowed a small part inside him to answer, but he refused to give Sepha anymore of himself. In answer, the demon viciously bit at Talah's throat and his talons slit Talah's skin open in their descent over his back. Talah had to force back his own reaction to the pain left in the wake of the slashes. He didn't want to give Sepha the satisfaction.

"You continue to refuse me, precious. I like the challenge."

Without warning, Talah found himself shoved face-first against the wall. One quick motion deprived him of his pants. He knew what was about to happen. A moment later Talah felt a mind-numbing pain as if he were being split in two.

CZ

The more time Talah spent with Sepha, the more obsessed the demon became in wanting to completely possess him. The only peaceful time Talah had was in the early evening. He spent every moment outside, either in the garden or wandering the city streets.

Leaning against the edge of a fountain, Talah crossed his legs and stretched them out in front of him. Earlier he'd overheard Oriyas telling Sepha that the Low Council had ordered him to release Talah. From the look on Sepha's face, it was clear the demon had no such intention. A smirk played over Talah's lips as he felt the warmth of the sun heating the garden. Unsure of exactly why Sepha had become obsessed with him, Talah still encouraged Sepha every way he could. It suited him for the time being to be kept and trained.

It certainly was a hell of a lot better than his time spent in the White Light. The same political backstabbing and overtones marred the foundations of the Damnation sect. However, Talah wasn't directly affected by them. The extent the Low Council wanted him to infiltrate the Order of the Highest, and that didn't truly interfere much with Talah. He didn't care either way.

His nights were more than pleasantly occupied by Sepha. The demon tended to occasionally use sex as a punishment, but it was nothing Talah couldn't handle. All in all, his life was quite comfortable. He had no doubt it would be the same once he went to the Order of the Highest. So either way, he couldn't lose.

Content for the most part as long as he continued to ignore the niggling sense inside him of being incomplete,

Talah relaxed. He nodded at Oriyas as the angel walked down the path toward him.

"You're getting to be entirely too much trouble around here." Oriyas' tone conveyed his disgust.

Talah smirked. "I'm not doing anything, and you know it."

"Get to the training room. Sepha is waiting for you." Clearly disgruntled, Oriyas whirled on his heel and stalked back into the house.

Talah shook his head. It hadn't been his fault that Sepha had decided to replace Oriyas. He knew the other demon had shared Sepha's bed before. No doubt Oriyas hoped with Talah gone, he would enjoy Sepha's affections again.

Leaving the garden, Talah headed back into the house. He passed through the opulent sapphire and gold study and walked down the hall to the training room. Talah couldn't care one way or the other who had prominence in Sepha's bed. While he greatly enjoyed the sex, he could get that anywhere. It might be a bit harder to find someone who liked it as rough as Sepha, but Talah was pretty damn easygoing in his sexual preferences.

When he entered the training room, Talah noticed Sepha wasn't standing by the arms rack like he usually was. Instead, he stood near the window, staring out at the garden. Quietly, Talah approached him then stopped.

"It seems I must release you." A grim smile creased Sepha's lips as he turned to face Talah. "You have been accepted into the Order of the Highest."

"It's the job you wanted me to do, Sepha." Talah remained where he stood, carefully studying the demon. He could sense Sepha's rage simmering just beneath the surface.

Sepha cupped Talah's chin, the tips of his talons pressing into the skin. "It is, and you are expected to report everything you learn to me. But don't forget, my precious, I own you. Have whatever fun you want elsewhere, but in the end, you will return to me." His fingers tightened, pulling Talah's face closer to his. "Should you forget, I will leave very little of you when I am done." Blood seeped from the wounds, but Talah didn't back away. He brought up his hand, fingers curling painfully tight around Sepha's wrist. "You don't own me yet, Sepha."

Releasing Talah, Sepha stepped back then in a flash of movement his talons slashed the young angel across the face. An enraged snarl escaped Talah as he struck back. His power might not be anywhere near Sepha's, but he retaliated nonetheless. Following in the wake of his fist, a bolt of energy seared through Sepha.

The force Sepha unleashed in return sent Talah flying against the wall of the training room. The impact cracked the plaster, leaving pieces on Talah's clothes as he slid to the floor.

Talah glared at Sepha before he abruptly disappeared. Wings outspread, Talah took to the air, moving through the layers of the house with ease. Once he was free of the house, Talah flew out over the city. He knew Sepha would catch up with him sooner or later and there'd be hell to pay, but he didn't care.

Chapter Two

Walking along the outer corridor, Talah knew his mentor had probably been watching him ever since he entered the compound. Since he'd only been allowed to see the lower echelon trainers, Talah wasn't sure who his mentor was.

After finishing his training exercises, he needed a relaxing shower and a few moments of rest. Dressed only in the loose white pants he'd donned for the training, Talah started for his room. Pushing open the door, Talah saw someone standing in the middle of the room. Talah stepped inside and closed the door behind him then paused, giving the other angel a questioning look.

"Ah, there you are." Eyes as fiery red as the angel's hair pinned a sharp gaze on Talah. "Sit, please." The angel gestured toward one of the couches.

Talah did as he was told. "Who are you? One of my new trainers?"

The angel waited until Talah was comfortable before speaking. "In a sense. My name is Aridas. How has your training progressed?"

Shrugging slightly, Talah folded his hands in his lap. "I haven't the same stamina as Ananiel, but I hold my own against him."

Aridas nodded. "That will change in time. And your studies, how do they fare?"

"Other than being bored, I'm doing very well. But you should ask Ipecis and see if she agrees." Talah had had more than a time or two of butting heads with his instructor.

One russet eyebrow rose. "I see. She can be...trying at times." Aridas settled on the corner of the large, polished wood desk, arms crossed over a muscular chest. "Now, tell me how you are doing otherwise."

Talah studied the long, lean form resting against his desk. How could he not help noticing the finest angel in the entire compound? Long, wavy red hair spilled down the angel's shoulders; the sparks lit within it from the light above caught Talah's gaze momentarily. "I am well taken care of, Aridas, and I lack for nothing."

"As your mentor, it is my duty to ensure that," Aridas said simply. "I will also be taking over your combat training, specifically archery, though I do teach hand-to-hand."

Looking directly into the red eyes, Talah smiled, a faint hint of suggestiveness in the gesture. "I look forward to that. I wondered when I would meet you."

Aridas seemed unmoved. "You will now occupy the room across from my chambers. My private office is just down the hall, and you are welcome there at any time.

Our first order of business..." He looked Talah up and down. "Yes, I think that will work. You need to build your upper strength. I expect you in the lower courtyard in fifteen minutes." With that, Aridas left.

Talah grabbed a towel and another pair of pants from his dresser then headed to the shower down the hall. After a quick wash, he dressed and made it down to the courtyard in under fifteen minutes. Not seeing Aridas, he stretched his wings restlessly.

A blur of motion was the only warning he had before the silver tip of an arrow touched Talah's right temple.

"Never let your guard down. That is your first lesson with me."

Snarling in surprise, Talah brought his hand up and hit Aridas' arm. Half twisting, he punched Aridas in the stomach, holding back none of his strength.

Aridas grunted but didn't show any reaction otherwise. "Very good," he said. "But you'll have to be quicker than that." In a flash of red light, he was gone. "Come on, Talah." The voice came from the rooftop of a storehouse across the courtyard. "You can do better than this. I've seen you."

Talah moved after him with a flex of his wings. No more than a split second later, he hovered over the roof, growling at Aridas before he swooped toward his mentor. Aridas dodged quickly. A hand shot out and caught Talah's right ankle, and Aridas tugged him down. Talah landed on his back, Aridas' arrow pointed at his throat.

"You are reckless."

Talah vowed to break that fucking arrow. He reached up and grabbed hold of Aridas' hand, but instead of trying to knock the arrow away as would be expected, Talah twisted the hand until the arrow pointed at Aridas.

"Interesting." Aridas smiled. He stepped back and offered Talah a hand up. "Time for you to learn how to shoot."

Talah got up and deliberately made sure he was close enough to Aridas to brush against him. "I try to be as interesting as I can."

Aridas didn't move away, nor did he let go of Talah's hand right away. "I imagine you do," he said quietly.

"And I can be even more interesting if you ever give me a chance."

"Can you, now?" Aridas' smile took on a different edge than that of a teacher.

Always one to take advantage wherever he could, Talah raised his face to his mentor. A second later, the warm brush of his lips touched Aridas' mouth. He really didn't care where they were or who saw them.

In the space of a breath, Talah found himself pinned against a wall, hidden in shadows as Aridas' tongue thrust between his lips. The angel's wings shielded them further, blocking all light. The kiss was hard, almost bruising. Talah found himself suddenly drowning in the unexpected hunger that sought to devour him.

Aridas was relentless. His body pressed tightly to Talah's, letting Talah feel every inch. Straining against Aridas, Talah was already aroused and could do nothing about it. Before he could stop it, Talah dropped his guard and answered the other angel far more openly than even he realized.

"I know you," Aridas whispered on Talah's lips. A steel grip seized Talah's wrists, pinning them to the wall above his head. "I see your dreams, Talah. I know you better than you know yourself."

Never having been in this position, Talah wasn't immediately sure how to react. Aridas made it nearly impossible for him to think. How had things switched and gotten out of his control? "You don't know me at all."

"Who is it you dream of in the dead of night?" Aridas' lips moved lower, sliding over the hollow of Talah's throat. "You long to meet your match."

Drawing in a quick, surprised breath, Talah couldn't answer right away. His hands flattened against Aridas and the first thing out of his mouth was denial. "I dream of no such thing."

Aridas' chuckle was deep. "Oh…" He slipped his hand between them, cupping the hard ridge of Talah's cock through his pants. "I think you do."

Talah growled softly in agitation and jerked one hand free. He covered Aridas' hand with his, but instead of pulling it away, he pressed it tighter to himself. Sensation shot straight through him and the growl became a soft groan. "You are playing me."

"And if I am?" Aridas' thumb ran along the length then back up to the tip, pressing hard.

"Just fuck me, Aridas."

Aridas licked his way up Talah's neck to his mouth. "As you wish." In a spark of red light they were indoors, and Aridas started backing Talah toward a bed. "I've watched you far too long to wait anymore for this." He pulled the tie on Talah's pants, letting them fall open.

With a tug of Talah's hand, Aridas' pants fell just as quickly. Stumbling back onto the bed, Talah pulled Aridas with him then stretched against the weight pinning him to the bed. Later he would ask for an explanation of Aridas' meaning, but right now he didn't care.

"Get yourself ready for me." Aridas placed a bottle of gold oil to Talah's palm.

Talah poured some of the oil onto his fingers and when Aridas rose, Talah rolled to his stomach then got onto his knees. He reached between his legs and pushed the slick fingers into himself. He knew Aridas watched him, and he made sure he put on quite a show.

"That's it," Aridas murmured, two fingers circling Talah's hole before entering alongside Talah's. "Show me you want it."

With a soft cry, Talah backed into the push of their fingers. A deep shudder rolled through him and his cock ached. "Inside me. Please, Aridas. I need it now."

Aridas withdrew his fingers then pulled Talah's hand away. He took only a brief moment to slick himself then he caught Talah's hips, tugging Talah back as he thrust deep in one swift movement. Talah cried out sharply and threw back his head, nails clawing into the covers beneath him.

Aridas wrapped a hand in Talah's hair and pulled him up. His chest to Talah's back and his cock buried deep, Aridas licked the curve of Talah's neck. "I know who you are," he whispered as he began rocking his hips slowly.

Talah didn't believe Aridas knew the full truth about him, otherwise he wouldn't be here in bed with the angel. Talah gripped Aridas' hip, grinding against the movement, so lost in the sensations he could barely gasp out, "You probably do."

A deep chuckle was Aridas' only answer. He released Talah's hair and cupped the front of Talah's neck. "So beautiful," he purred softly. The words were followed by a slow grind of his hips, his cock grazing over Talah's gland. "So certain."

"I knew I wanted you the moment I saw you," Talah groaned, using his other hand to stroke himself.

Aridas withdrew and stretched out on his back. He held out his hand to Talah. "Ride me. I want everything, Talah."

Talah twisted around and straddled Aridas. His wings unfurled to their full glory as he lowered himself back onto Arida's cock. The light shimmered within the violet depths of the feathers with his movements. He didn't have much other than his body to give Aridas, but he was very willing to do that.

Aridas traced the bottom edge of Talah's left wing. "Perfection..."

A low sound rose in Talah's throat, betraying the effect Aridas had on him. Slowly, he ground his hips against Aridas. One hand fisted over his own cock as the other kneaded into Aridas' chest. Talah badly wanted a kiss and leaned down to take it. The soft touch of his lips covered the angel's, and his tongue parted Aridas' lips.

Aridas opened, sucking Talah's tongue into his mouth. He drew up his feet and rolled his hips, pushing as he pulled Talah down. Moaning into the kiss, he slid his other hand along the back of Talah's right wing, fingers stroking the feathers.

Several shudders rolled through Talah with Aridas' caress. Unable to keep to the slower pace, Talah rode Aridas harder and faster. The need for release overwhelmed Talah, and the motion of his hand quickened. The bruising kiss muffled his cry as he came, spilling onto Aridas' stomach.

With a deep groan, Aridas thrust up hard, hips slamming against Talah as he filled Talah with his release. He nipped Talah's bottom lip as he slowly ended the kiss. "Why are you really here?"

Talah collapsed against Aridas, his senses scattered. "I am here to learn from the Order, to train."

Aridas hummed his agreement, though there was a touch of disbelief in it. "I see." He rolled them, putting Talah beneath him. "I requested you the moment I knew of your impending arrival. Did you know that?"

"Why?"

"Let us just say..." Aridas drew Talah's arms above Talah's head, pressing them to the pillow. "...that I've been watching you for quite some time. Long before you came here."

"Watching me?" Talah tensed before he realized that Aridas' couldn't have caught him doing anything serious. "I can't imagine why you would."

"You're quite out of place here. Or have you not noticed?" Aridas stroked his fingers over Talah's palm, stopping only when he reached the pulse point of Talah's wrist.

"I'm out of place everywhere. Of course, I've noticed. But I need to be trained, so it doesn't matter."

One eyebrow rose, but Aridas didn't release him. "Why bring the wars here?"

Startled, Talah frowned at him. "I have done no such thing. What are you accusing me of?"

"I am not accusing. I am questioning." Aridas' hand returned to pin Talah's wrist down. "Leaving the Order of White Light is no small feat. No one just leaves. Who sent you here?"

"It is when the internal problems within the order interfere in my training. I have every right to request additional training from another order, Aridas. If you are suspicious of me, why have you allowed me into your bed?"

"I will not refuse you training," Aridas said sternly, "but I will do it under my own discretions. This is my institute, my Order. I make the rules. As for why you are here..." He smirked and rocked his hips, his newly hardened cock sliding in and out of Talah. "I take what I want."

Closing his eyes, Talah rocked against the motion. Aridas proved to be a huge distraction. Something Talah wasn't sure if he could afford or not. But the thought couldn't take hold with the need already filling him. "I just want you to fuck me."

Bracing his knees on the bed, Aridas thrust forward, pinning Talah's hands down as he kissed Talah hard. Legs encircling Aridas, Talah writhed beneath the forceful fucking. He was being thoroughly used and enjoyed every minute of it. His fingers curled tightly around Aridas' hand as his mouth tightened around the angel's tongue.

Aridas broke the kiss and descended on Talah's neck, sucking hard. He slammed his hips into Talah, biting down on his throat as the thrusts grew in strength. "Come."

The one word command took over Talah's mind, and his body strained from the bed before a violent shaking overtook him. Something seemed to fill him from Aridas, but Talah couldn't comprehend exactly what had happened as he fell over the edge, yelling incoherently.

Aridas smiled against Talah's neck, and with one last stroke, he came, pumping heat deep inside Talah's body. "Let the Disillusioned break that one."

Half sobbing, Talah was completely overwhelmed. He had no idea what happened, his wits too scattered for once to form anything coherent.

"Shh, I've got you." Aridas eased out and rolled to the side. One wing came up and covered them. Aridas drew Talah close.

"I've never experienced..."

"I know," Aridas whispered.

Chapter Three

Though he tried to keep his attention on the monotonous drone of the meeting, Aridas found his thoughts drifting away, back to Talah as they tended to lately. Despite knowing Talah was a fallen angel, Aridas couldn't help the need that filled him whenever Talah was near. He'd felt the undeniable pull on his soul the moment Talah had entered his domain. The question now was, who was the young, impressionable demon working for?

"The Order of the Lowest Creation has requested additional training at our facility for two of their novices. Are our trainers equipped to handle two more trainees?" Enael read over the report in his hand then glanced up at the others.

"I wouldn't see a problem taking on one of them, Enael. As long as their level is sufficiently high enough. Both Talah and Ephias are proving to be quick at their studies, but the other three are a little more slow-going." Tern set down his cup as he checked through his list. "I don't see a way to fit in the other one. At least for me."

"Kalios is free," Aridas said, half-surprised that he'd managed to keep up with the topic at all. "Send the other to her."

Nodding, Enael made a note on the report. "How is Talah working out?" He glanced up, pinning Aridas with a knowing—and slightly amused—look.

"He is doing very well," Aridas answered dryly.

Ignoring the undertone, Tern continued looking over his list. "Zalon and Btakit can handle their physical training."

Enael eyed Aridas for a moment longer before he spoke, "We have seven more requests coming in soon. I'd like to have everything prepared to handle them, Tern. Check with the trainers and see which ones will be available."

Aridas returned his old friend's gaze. "If that is all, gentlemen?"

Both Tern and Enael nodded.

"Very good. Let me know when the new arrivals are situated so that I can update my records. In the meantime, have a good day." With that, Aridas stood and left the room. He had work to be done, but the urge to find Talah remained strong. So strong, in fact, that Aridas bypassed his chamber door without fully realizing it.

Stepping out into the bright day, he ignored the others training in various skills throughout the yard. Aridas closed his eyes and let his mind settle. Though it was still weak, he found the thread connecting him to Talah. His mind followed it, the landscape sliding by in perfect clarity. When he realized where Talah was, Aridas barely bit back the possessive growl. His wings unfurled and he took to the sky, heading for the small town of Ethelene, and its less-than-reputable districts.

CS

Talah sprawled easily in the booth, finding quite a few of the others around him to be very entertaining. Though most liquors didn't affect him, he'd treated himself to a special bottle of an extremely potent mixture that would.

A young man approached him and motioned to the dance floor. In the mood for a bit of gaiety, Talah nodded and stood. As the music started, a pair of arms wrapped around him and a warm body pressed lightly up against his.

"Haven't seen you here before," the man said with a seductive smile. "What's your name?"

"Talah. And yours?"

"Relai." Hardness pressed against Talah's thigh as Relai swayed to the music, never breaking contact between them. "What do you want tonight? I'm skilled in many forms of pleasure."

"I can't say that I'm looking for anything in particular, Relai." Draping one arm over Relai's shoulder, Talah encircled the young man's waist with the other. "What are you looking for? Besides money?"

Relai's wicked grin spread slowly. "To give you the

best night of your life."

Feeling an odd sort of tingling across his senses, Talah scanned the room. His startled gaze met a very unhappy pair of blazing red eyes staring right at him. Leaning toward Relai, he whispered, "You might want to leave now."

With a surprised look, Relai stepped back then seemed to take Talah at his word as he retreated to the bar.

Without saying a word, Aridas reached out and seized Talah's wrist, jerking Talah hard against him. "I don't share."

The hard feel of Aridas' body set off an instant chain reaction within Talah, though Talah struggled against it. "I didn't realize I belonged to you, Aridas."

"I'm sure you didn't." A soft growl followed, Aridas' mouth crashing down on Talah's without warning.

Talah gave up the fight and snaked his arms around Aridas as the angel demanded entry. Aridas thrust his tongue into Talah's mouth, the kiss hard and insistent. Aridas slid one hand down to grip Talah's hip, while his other hand cupped the back of Talah's head. Fingers tangled in his hair as Aridas deepened the kiss.

Light flashed and surrounded them and, seconds later, Talah's back hit a wall. Aridas pinned him tight, breathing "Say it" on Talah's lips.

Bemused, Talah could only gasp in answer. He'd been so lost in what had risen in him, he had no clue what Aridas wanted. "Don't let me go. Please, Aridas."

"If you think I intend to..." Aridas tore Talah's pants down the front. "...you are sadly mistaken."

Unknowing and uncaring of where they were, Talah pulled off his tunic then tried to press closer to Aridas. He could feel the hard line of the angel's cock encased in his pants, and the grinding of his hips trapped their cocks together. "Need you in me."

Spinning Talah around, Aridas shoved him toward a set of stairs. They were back home, in a deserted, familiar hallway. "Up. I expect you to be ready for me."

Talah unfurled his wings and climbed the stairs. He'd already been in Aridas' private chambers once, so he knew where the bedroom was. Picking up a small jar from the stand near the bed, Talah opened it as he slid onto the bed. He remained on his hands and knees and parted his legs for Aridas.

After he slicked two of his fingers, he lowered his hand between his legs then pushed into his hole. Slowly he fucked himself and when he looked over his shoulder, he saw the angel standing in the doorway, staring unblinkingly at him.

"It feels so fucking good to have something inside me," Talah moaned. "Want it to be you."

Without looking away, Aridas undressed slowly, stalking toward the bed. "By all means," he purred as his pants slipped to the floor, "tell me more."

Talah continued to fuck himself as his gaze followed Aridas. The rhythm of his heart oddly began to beat in sync with Aridas' movements, and he could feel the strengthening of his need for the man coming closer to him. "Please, Aridas. It has to be you."

Aridas stilled by the bed and reached out, fingers sliding down Talah's spine. Without warning, he lifted his hand and delivered a firm slap to Talah's ass. "So sweet..."

Talah squirmed with the smack, and the motion of his fingers quickened. His breath caught in his throat before he got out the angel's name again. "Aridas."

Aridas traced the fingers of his other hand down Talah's back as he knelt behind him then pushed two slowly inside Talah. "Liked that, did you?" Aridas whispered, landing a second sharp smack to Talah's ass.

Groaning with the second hit, Talah arched toward Aridas' hands. He gripped the posts tightly. The roll of his hips fucked the angel's fingers, sending sensation after sensation rippling through him. He wanted to reach for his cock, but forcefully kept his hands where they were.

"Very good," Aridas breathed in Talah's ear. "Ride my fingers. Show me how much you want it." Aridas added a third finger, spreading them apart.

Talah's nails dug into the wood as the ache of his cock and the stretching inside him drove him crazy. The hard push of his ass drove the fingers deeper and Talah shuddered with the rubbing friction across his gland. Desperately, he cried out.

In one breath, Aridas' cock replaced his fingers and he thrust hard. "Do not come," he commanded, pumping in and out of Talah with hard, deep strokes.

Talah couldn't breathe; the burning stretch overwhelmed him. As everything built within him, Talah held onto the post, coming close to breaking the wood. He pushed back into every thrust, and his moan took on a sharper intensity.

The strength of Aridas' strokes increased, his hips slamming hard against Talah. Wrapping a hand in Talah's hair, Aridas rammed into him and growled, "Come."

The one word sent a tremor racing through Talah and a second later, he obeyed. His sharp cry of pleasure filled the room and the angel's name fell from his lips.

Aridas groaned, hips rocking, pumping his cock in and out. "Make no mistake," he growled as he shot. "You are mine."

Part of Talah already understood, but it was a part he refused to acknowledge. He leaned heavily against the post, bowing his head as he tried to regain his senses. Placing a kiss on Talah's neck, Aridas withdrew slowly.

"Come on. Time for sleep." Aridas urged Talah down to the bed with him.

Aridas made him incapable of any real thought. Without protest, Talah nuzzled as close as he could to the angel and closed his eyes. The only place he could feel this way was near Aridas. At times it confused him, but more and more he came to accept it.

C8

Sitting at his desk, the book open in front of him, Talah heard only half of what Tern was going on about.

"Each Order has its place within the entire order of the universe. Though some Orders aren't as prominent as others, each serves creation in its own unique way. As the Order of the Highest, we serve the other Orders in their need for highly specialized training. Some of our novices return to their own Orders and some make a choice to remain with us."

"Talah, what is the duty of the White Light?"

Roused from his thoughts, Talah answered promptly. "To serve the souls of the inhabitants of the first planet of the universe."

"Quite right. And even though there is internal strife within the Order itself, it will never interfere in the prime duty of the White Light."

Talah wasn't so sure about that, but he remained silent.

"Ephias, what is the duty of the Order of Destruction?"

"To destroy those who have fallen from the original plan of creation."

"Correct. Over existence many have fallen away from the original plan of creation. The Faction of the Disillusioned contains many different sects. You all know the history of the original Fall, but it continues even now. Hopefully none but Ephias will come into contact with any Disillusioned, but knowledge of them would still be helpful." Tern paused, eyeing each of his students in turn before he continued. "There is a list of three books I want everyone to read. You will find them in the compound library."

Since he already knew a considerable amount about both sides, Talah only half listened to Tern's lecture. He knew the hierarchy of the angels: Michael at the top, and Adonai, Gabriel, Uriel and Raphael on the second tier. Then those they had trained were of the third tier, though all of those names had never been listed. The Disillusioned had the same hierarchy but with Lucifer at its head.

Angels were members of Orders and the fallen were members of Faction subsects. It seemed somewhat ironic that the demons held to the same structure they'd lived before they'd become fallen. Talah himself was of the fallen, though only by choice. He hadn't been part of the original Fall, and a large number of the Disillusioned weren't either. They'd been created after it.

Watching Tern as if he were actually paying attention, Talah stifled a yawn. He managed to sit still until the lesson was over. After Tern dismissed them, Talah headed upstairs for a short break before he had to be at the outside training area.

Once alone in his room, he disrobed and quickly bathed in the pool. Even though he would be training in another hour, he'd needed the bath since he had spent most of the earlier day training as well. He dried off then stretched out over the soft covers of his bed.

Focusing on his body, he began to relax each group of

muscles to ease any lingering tension. There was only one place he wanted to feel any tightness, and his hand circled his cock, running up and down the length in varying strokes. Talah centered himself on the beginning ache as it spread from his cock outward.

A soft groan escaped him as his hips began jerking up, thrusting his cock against his hand. He kept the timing slow and torturous, delaying the inevitable to strengthen it. Thoughts filled his head with images of Aridas and him together, and a deeper moan rose in his throat along with the angel's name.

Unable to control the sudden rush of heated need that swept him, Talah tightened his hand around his cock. His hips rose, desperately fucking the air, begging for the feel of the cock he wanted so badly. When he came, he called out repeatedly to Aridas, barely aware of the sound of his own voice. Finally collapsing back to the bed, Talah became annoyed with himself.

He didn't have time for daydreams about Aridas. Growling, he sat up and wiped himself off with the edge of the blanket. "I've got to get myself together. I'm nothing more than a passing fancy to Aridas."

A vague sense of hurt started to rise in him, but Talah stood, mentally shaking it off. Nothing mattered but what he had to do.

CB

"Who is he, really?"

Aridas didn't look at Tern, choosing instead to watch Talah train out in the courtyard. "I have a good idea, but I won't say anything further until I have answers."

Tern stepped beside him and looked down at the young fallen angel. "Are you so certain he will tell you?"

"In time," Aridas said quietly as he studied the sleek, graceful movements of Talah's wings. He could watch Talah forever. Shaking his head to clear his thoughts, he smiled over at his friend. "I have my ways of persuasion."

Tern glanced at him and smirked. "So I've noticed. Really, Aridas, must you play with him before he attends my class? His attention is already scattered enough as is."

It felt good to laugh, and Aridas just shook his head. "Look at him, Tern." He waved toward the window. Talah was sparring with another angel, the sword sparkling in the sunlight. "Can you resist such temptation?"

"I prefer the fairer ones."

Aridas chuckled as Tern clapped him on the back before walking out. Turning his attention back to the action below, Aridas thought on how much his life had changed since Talah wandered into it. He'd had such a handle on things before, rarely lost his temper, and he certainly never enjoyed his students the way he enjoyed Talah. The proof of his suspicions was right there, whether he wanted to admit it or not.

Every soul has its twin—light for dark, dark for light. As he stood there at the window, gazing down at the sight of Talah parrying and thrusting his sword, Aridas knew he could no longer run away from the truth.

Talah was his twin, the dark to his light.

Chapter Four

For two weeks Aridas allowed Talah to remain secretive about his identity, but it was time to end it. There was too much at stake—for himself and the Order—for Aridas to let Talah keep quiet. He found Talah on the archery range. The fallen angel's aim had greatly improved from when he'd first arrived. Aridas leaned back against the wall, arms crossed as he watched Talah intently.

As he nocked the arrow to the bow, Talah stiffened. Then he drew back the arrow and let it fly. It hit the target off to the side of the center. Clearly something had disturbed his concentration. Frowning, Talah handed the bow to his trainer then listened before he nodded. Talah headed back into the compound in the opposite direction.

Aridas trailed behind Talah. He caught the door to Talah's room just before it closed. "You can't avoid me forever."

"Why not?" Talah stilled beside his dresser. Not bothering to look at Aridas, he opened one of the drawers and pulled out another set of clothes.

"Because it is futile, especially here." Aridas closed the door, taking care to lock it. "Sit. We have much to discuss."

Tossing the shirt and pants on top of the dresser, Talah stared at him for a long moment before he finally sat on the edge of the bed. "What do we have to discuss?"

"How about you start with the truth? It will be much easier that way."

"What truth?"

"I'm done playing games, Talah. If you don't tell me willingly then I will force it out of you."

Talah stood abruptly. "Look, I don't know what you're talking about, Aridas. It's time for me to meet with Tern."

"Report to my office when you are done." Within the blink of an eye, Aridas was gone.

Ignoring his own bad feeling, Talah changed his clothes before he left the room. It only took him a moment to get to the Order's library. Looking around, he saw Tern hadn't shown up yet, so he headed down one of the aisles to get a head start on the books he needed. He pulled one of the books from the shelf and leafed through it. He could hear the voice of others entering the library, but he didn't pay much attention to them.

"Did Sipiel speak to you yet, Enael?"

"Yes. But he wasn't sure what the trouble was about." The sound of books landing on a table followed.

"Aridas has been short of temper lately and it's not like him."

Talah looked up from the book and moved closer to the voices, taking care not to be seen.

"Anything that bothers our leader is bound to be a great deal of trouble, Aseron."

The comment hit Talah like a blow. His mentor was the leader of the Order of the Highest. Disbelief kept him frozen as the other two walked off. When he could move, he headed around the bookshelves back into the central area of the library. The book was nearly forgotten in his hand.

"Ah, there you are." Tern appeared at the end of the aisle. "Did you find the books on my list?"

"Uh, yes, I found one of them, Tern."

"Wonderful. One of them is in Aridas' office. Though, when you go to get it, be aware, he's been in a mood lately."

"It would be," Talah muttered under his breath. "I'll take this back to my room and get the other book as well. Did you need me for anything else?"

Tern thought for a moment. "Oh. Yes. Taleon sent word for you to be in his office in one hour."

"Why am I popular all of a sudden?"

Tern shrugged. "Beats me. Get that book from Aridas, though, and get yourself to Taleon's office." With that, Tern left the library.

Talah put down the book. Not about to ignore his sense of inner alarm, he strode to the door and looked out. Instead of heading for the upstairs offices, he walked to the outer door of the building and went outside.

Once he was free and clear of the structure, his wings unfurled and he took flight. He had to get back to Sepha before any of the Order got their hands on him. In a blur of speed, distance displaced for him, and when it slowed he landed on one of the streets of Nara. Making his way to the nearby bar, Talah pushed opened the door. No doubt Sepha would show up sooner or later, and Talah was prepared to wait for him.

"What can I get ya?" a woman asked as she approached him just as he sat at one of the tables.

"A bottle of your strongest stuff." Talah knew Sepha wouldn't be at home right now. The demon was normally out recruiting through the area with Oriyas, but Talah had little doubt they would eventually come into the bar.

"On the way, hun." She headed off to the bar.

The door opened a moment later and a hooded, cloaked figure walked in. No one seemed to notice the newcomer as the figure went to a table in a dark corner. When another woman approached the stranger, there were hushed voices, a nod of her head, and she left the table again.

Talah kept an eye on the door, but ignored the stranger for the most part as he waited for his drink. Before the barmaid could return, Sepha came in. Immediately Sepha's golden gaze found him.

"What are you doing here, my sweet?" Sepha purred.

Keeping his voice low, Talah got right to the point. "I've had a problem, Sepha. I believe they've somehow discovered who I am."

"You will explain everything to me later." Sepha paused when Oriyas walked up to the table. "It seems my young one has returned to us unexpectedly."

"What happened?" Oriyas asked.

"They know who I am," Talah said.

Oriyas lifted an eyebrow. "How?"

Sepha cupped Talah's face in his hand, his talons sharp, digging into Talah's skin as Sepha pulled him closer. From the look in Sepha's eyes, Talah hazarded a guess that the demon might know more than Talah wanted him to.

"My precious Talah will tell me all about it later, won't you?" Not letting Talah answer, Sepha kissed him hard.

When the barmaid set down several mugs in the center of the table, Sepha pulled back and smirked. He lifted his mug and took a healthy swallow. "Return to the house. You will explain everything there." Finishing off his drink, Sepha stood. "I expect you there promptly."

Oriyas got up as well and followed. "Do you want me to handle Isasen?"

"No, we will both take care of him then I will return home," Sepha answered before directing a look back at Talah. His faint smile spoke volumes.

After drinking half of his cup, Talah set it down then slid out of the booth to leave as well.

Sepha and Oriyas made it out the door, but just before Talah neared it, the cloaked figure shimmered into form before him. "Upstairs. Now."

Recognizing the voice, Talah stiffened, but before he could get away, a relentless grip encircled his arm. He had no choice but to follow as Aridas pulled him up the stairs and down the hall to one of the private rooms. The second Aridas locked the door, he slammed Talah face-first against it.

"Leaving was a very stupid idea."

Pain shot through Talah as his face pressed into the wood. He growled and twisted, freeing his arm, and went for Aridas. He had no doubt the angel planned to kill him.

An iron grip seized his arms, wrenching both behind Talah's back. Aridas used his free hand to rip Talah's pants open. "You came into my House under false pretense," he snarled. Hard, heated flesh slid between Talah's thighs. "But you made one very bad mistake..." Two barely-slick fingers thrust into Talah. Aridas' voice dropped to a whisper. "You left."

Shock rippled through Talah. He hadn't expected this at all. Before he could subdue his own response, a low moan escaped him. "Aridas."

Withdrawing his hand, Aridas spit on his palm, slicked his cock and pushed in, filling and stretching Talah without stopping. His entire length buried deep inside, Aridas pinned Talah to the wall, one hand reaching around between Talah's body and the wooden wall to wrap tight around his prick. "Don't do it again."

Talah was lost and he knew it. He had no resistance to Aridas. The pressure filled him and his thoughts spun wildly out of control. "Fuck me, Aridas. Let me feel you again."

"If I see him near you again, I will kill him," Aridas snarled in Talah's ear, his thrusts brutal as he pumped in and out of Talah's body.

Talah realized what had brought this out in the angel. He met each thrust, wallowing in the roughness as he reached back for Aridas. He could feel Aridas everywhere inside him. It felt as if Aridas had taken complete possession of him, and Talah gave in to it. "I just want you."

"Prove it." Aridas stopped moving. "Come."

The echo of Aridas' voice ran deep inside Talah. Before he could still or control it, the sudden urge overwhelmed him. Without even touching himself, he began to shake and he cried out to his lover as he came.

"Where do you belong?"

Collapsing back against Aridas, Talah shivered uncontrollably. He knew the answer and could no longer deny it. "With you."

Aridas pulled out slowly then slammed back inside, hips jerking as light exploded around them, fusing their souls.

Blinded by the energy, Talah felt the piercing heat envelop him. Within it, he felt nothing but Aridas. He didn't even hear his own cry as tears rolled unheeded down his cheeks. He'd been brought home, where he belonged.

Easing out, Aridas drew Talah back toward the bed.

"Shhh, I'm here." He got them on the bed and held Talah close.

"I work for the Damnation sect, Aridas. They sent me to the Order of the Highest to gain information about your Order."

"I wondered if they might be behind it. Thank you for telling me, Talah." Aridas slipped a finger beneath Talah's chin. "You will be safe with me, but only if you do not keep secrets anymore. If there's more I need to know, tell me. I know the being you spoke with earlier, but by reputation only. Anything more you can tell me will help us both."

"Sepha is the leader. Originally, he wanted me in your Order. Then he decided to keep me, and the Low Council demanded he send me on my mission. I don't really know that much about him."

"What is he up to?" Aridas mused quietly.

"I don't really know. He never told me. But I don't think he'll let go of me easily. You've seen what he's like."

"I have, unfortunately. Sepha is a warmonger, Talah. I wouldn't put anything of that magnitude past him."

"We probably shouldn't stay here long. He's going to come looking for me once he finds out I'm not home." Talah tried to get out of the bed so they could leave.

"In a minute." Aridas stopped him, rolling half on top of Talah. "I want a kiss first."

Finding himself pinned back to the bed, Talah draped his arms over Aridas' shoulders. He lifted his head, covering Aridas' lips, and parted them with his tongue. In

169

the kiss, he tried to express all he could of his own growing need for the angel.

Licking Talah's lips, Aridas pulled back slowly. "Now we can go."

Talah wanted Aridas' hands on him and he arched against him. "In a minute we can."

Aridas chuckled, hand sliding down, fingers closing around Talah's cock. "What do you want, Talah?"

"To always be a part of you."

"You always will be." Aridas slid down and traced the length of Talah's cock with his tongue.

Talah parted his legs for Aridas, giving the angel access to him. Drawing up his knees, Talah rolled his hips, urging Aridas to do more. Aridas rolled the lower half of Talah's body upward. Then Aridas flicked his tongue over Talah's hole, never breaking eye contact.

"Please, Aridas, please."

Aridas lowered him and, with Talah slick with spit, he thrust his cock inside in one smooth motion. "Come on," he whispered, leaning down to lick Talah's lips, "take what you want."

Talah wrapped his legs around Aridas and met the angel's movements, stroke for stroke. He bit at Aridas' lower lip hard enough to draw blood then licked away the few drops.

"I want everything." Aridas rolled them until Talah was on top. Gripping Talah's hips, he thrust up, pushing his cock deeper.

Giving Aridas what he asked for, Talah spread his violet wings out. The movement of his hips continuously impaled him on Aridas' cock as Talah's nails lengthened then ran downward over the angel's chest.

"Take me…" With the words, Aridas turned his head, baring his neck in invitation.

"I give it all to you." His true nature began to show as he lowered his head to Aridas' throat. This was something he'd never done for anyone, yet Talah willingly did it for Aridas. Talah sank his teeth into the tender flesh and drank greedily. Talah's climax surprised him, wave after wave rolling over him in exquisite pleasure.

"Talah." Aridas whispered the name seconds before heat rushed through them both, his body arching beneath Talah's as he came.

They both remained joined together as Talah continued taking Aridas' blood. When everything slowly returned to normal, Talah released him. Lifting his head, he licked at the drops of blood left on them as he stared down at Aridas. "I will always hunger for you."

"And I will always be here to sate that hunger."

"I know that somehow, but we really should leave now."

"I agree." Talah got off the bed and picked up the remnants of his pants. "I suppose I should be grateful my tunic covers everything."

Aridas chuckled and dressed. "Sorry about that. I'll make sure you have replacements when we return to the Order."

Talah dropped the pants with a shrug. "Come on. Let's get out of here."

"Right behind you."

Chapter Five

Though he'd returned to the Order with Aridas, Talah found it hard to stay behind the cloistered walls. Slipping out to the nearby town, he strolled down the crowded street, simply enjoying the noise and the bustle. Cutting down one of the alleys, he ignored the filth strewn on the ground. He was in the mood for a drink or two at one of the nearby taverns then he planned on returning to the Order before anyone noticed he was gone.

Lost in his own thoughts, Talah paid little attention to his surroundings. Lately everything he thought about revolved around Aridas. He wasn't sure how to explain any of it, except he felt whole with the angel in his life, something he never felt before. Knowing Aridas' emotions were the same was something Talah had yet to adjust to.

Even away from the protected walls of the Order, Talah could feel Aridas within him. It was as if the angel's power shadowed him. Nothing in his existence had prepared Talah for his own emotions or dealing with another who needed him. But it felt so easy just to slip into it, to allow it to be. Talah hadn't struggled against any of it, and he had no intention of even trying to.

A shadowed figure jumped down from the roof of a nearby building and landed near Talah. Before Talah could react, a numbing force took over his body. He remained standing but couldn't move at all.

Sepha straightened from his crouch then grabbed Talah, pulling the angel against him. "You tried to escape me, my little pet."

Talah was given no chance to answer as they took to the air. In a dizzying blur, they set down on the floor of Sepha's main salon.

"Now explain to me why you didn't return to me as I told you."

The moment Talah could move, he attacked Sepha, expending what energy he could.

Sepha's talons sank into Talah's face and arm. He shoved Talah back and kept the angel pinned against the wall with his body. "Did you really think I would let you go free?"

Talah stared unblinkingly at him, ignoring the blood dripping from the wounds. "You don't own me."

"You're mated with that bastard. That's why you went with him, isn't it?" Pure rage twisted Sepha's features, and his talons tore into Talah's chest.

Talah couldn't react as a brutal force freed him from the talons and sent him flying toward the ceiling as Sepha cursed him. "You worthless whelp! I own you!"

Before he could fall, Talah hung spread eagle, suspended in mid air. Sepha lifted his hand, engulfing Talah in hellfire. "I've only played with you before, my precious. Now you will truly feel what I can do."

Talah's mind blanked as he writhed in the agonizing pressure. Bereft in the excruciating torment, Talah screamed.

Thunder shook the walls so strongly that Sepha's concentration was broken. Growling, he spun around seconds before a blast of white light slammed him back against the opposite wall. A blur of red and orange followed, and several arrows found their targets in Sepha's chest and shoulders.

Blood poured from Talah's mouth, nose and eyes to the floor beneath him. The hellfire left his body misshapen and distorted. He fell to the floor and lay in a heap. Sepha roared. His body ejected the arrows as he advanced on Talah.

Light enveloped Talah, protecting him from anything Sepha might have done. The figure in the doorway stepped into the room, red eyes blazing with fury. A lift of the angel's hand had Sepha flying through the air again, pinning him to the wall near the ceiling.

"You should know better, Sepha."

Sepha's power pushed back against the force that held him to the wall and he dropped to his feet. A split second later, he flew through the air straight at Aridas and sent the angel back through the door. Their bodies tangled as Sepha's talons sank into Aridas. "You. So you are the one."

Aridas heaved Sepha off of him. "Such a pleasure."

Sepha got back onto his feet in the blink of an eye

and whirled to face Aridas. "My claim is first on him."

Talah tried to get up on his hands and knees, attempting to focus on the other two.

"Mine is stronger," Aridas countered. "If you want Talah that badly then you will have to kill me first."

A simple look from Sepha sent Talah collapsing back to the floor. The pain, while not as agonizing as before, debilitated the young angel.

Smirking at Aridas, Sepha laughed before he said, "And I control him."

With only a slight bit of power, Aridas began healing Talah's wounds, siphoning some of his strength to aid Talah. "He bows to me willingly."

"You can no more destroy me than I can destroy you, Aridas." Sepha crouched in front of Talah. "And it seems we wish to possess the same toy. A problem, wouldn't you say?"

With the added strength, Talah's wings spread out in agitation as he half rose to his knees then struck out at Sepha. Easily blocking the blow, Sepha twisted them both until they were facing Aridas. His arm pinned Talah against him as he lowered his head, savagely biting the angel's throat. Gloating triumph gleamed in the gaze that held Aridas.

His expression deathly calm, Aridas drew an arrow from his second quiver. Drawing the bow, he said, "A problem indeed." Then he let the arrow fly.

An unearthly shriek filled the room as the arrow drove deep into Sepha's forehead. He reared back, clawing ineffectually at it. The power infusing the arrow ate like acid over the outer shell of Sepha's form. The scream stopped abruptly and a few seconds later, the demon's body dissolved into dust.

Talah swayed on his knees, trying to reach out for Aridas. His body had already begun to heal, but his energy had been severely disrupted. Aridas caught him before he could hit the floor.

"Come on. Let's get out of here."

When Aridas picked him up, Talah tried to burrow against him, his arms circling in a death hold around the angel's neck. "I'm sorry...I'm sorry."

"Shh..." Aridas got them out of the house and once outside, took to the air. "Not your fault, Talah. You're safe now."

"You destroyed him. How did you destroy him?"

"Like me, Sepha cannot be destroyed. His soul returns to the ether to be reborn. Only the outer shell that housed him is gone." Aridas set them down in front of the Order's great hall. "But it will take a lifetime for him to return."

"What did you use on him?" Talah asked as they went to Aridas' chambers within the Order.

"One of my gifts—the best, I dare say—are my enchanted arrows." Aridas closed the door and locked it behind them. "Forged from lightning, they're the ones I reserve for desperate times. We'll get you cleaned up. Are you all right otherwise?"

"Other than wishing I hadn't snuck out for a bit of

fun, I think I'm fine." Although his body had been restored, Talah wouldn't soon forget exactly what Sepha could do. He stepped back from Aridas and peeled the tattered clothing from his body.

Aridas helped him, the touches gentle. "I wish I had gotten there sooner. I'm sorry, Talah."

"That wasn't your fault. If anything I shouldn't have snuck out. I didn't think he would dare come that close to the Order's territory."

"Neither did I."

Once Talah undressed, Aridas led him into a small room with a pool inset into the stone floor. He helped Talah down into the heated water then sat on the edge, watching him.

"In all truth, I cannot hold you here against your will," Aridas said quietly.

Talah sank into the water and its warmth surrounded him, easing the tension. Looking up at Aridas, he shook his head vehemently. "I'm not here against my will. I'm here because..." He trailed off, momentarily startled. "I'm here because I am a part of you."

Aridas reached out, smiling as a lock of hair wound around his finger of its volition. "As I am a part of you."

"We belong together. What Sepha wanted, I've given to you. And he knew that. I didn't know at first, but now I know I'm not empty inside anymore."

"We are two halves of the same soul, Talah. We were created from the same bit of ether, formed to be twins on opposite sides of the spectrum."

178

"For the first time, I believe in that, Aridas." Talah soaped off the blood and rinsed beneath the water. When he emerged, he pushed his hair out of his face as he approached Aridas.

"It amazes me how you managed to get through this old man's defenses..." Aridas muttered.

"I'm not entirely sure how that happened." Talah shivered beneath the lovingly lustful look directed at him. Leaning against the edge of the pool, he slipped his arms around Aridas' neck. "At first I thought you were just going to be another enjoyable fuck."

Aridas' clothes dissolved into the ether and he slipped into the water, hands resting on Talah's hips. "And now?"

"Now? There isn't a part of me that doesn't belong to you. It scares me in a way, but I need you too much to be without you." Talah rubbed against Aridas, slowly arousing both of them.

Aridas tipped Talah's head back, licking a line up the middle of his throat. "Love..."

"Always." Closing his eyes, Talah became pliable in Aridas' arms. There wasn't anything Talah wouldn't let the angel do.

"Complete this," Aridas whispered, lips brushing Talah's neck just below his left ear. "Complete the circle, Talah."

Talah groaned softly, realizing what Aridas wanted. "I want you on the bed."

"Yes." Aridas' wings unfurled, lifting them from the water. Setting them at the foot of the bed, Aridas didn't hide his wings, simply letting them rest, water still dripping from the dark orange feathers.

Talah planned on taking things very slowly to savor everything to the fullest. The soft brush of his lips touched the angel's then teased over them before his tongue coaxed a soft sound of need from Aridas. The simple touch seemed to be Aridas' undoing. He shivered and pressed closer, drawing Talah's tongue into his mouth, sucking lightly on it as his hands rested on Talah's shoulders, fingers kneading into the skin. Talah bore Aridas down onto the bed and knelt between the angel's legs. He lowered his head, licking a line over the length of Aridas' cock before lifting the angel's hips.

"Talah..." The name was whispered. Aridas' normally stern and stoic demeanor crumbled, became wanton and needy.

Having Aridas literally in the palms of his hands was an erotic rush all on its own. Talah teased beneath Aridas' balls with his tongue as his fingers cupped and massaged them. Moving lower, he slowly rimmed the outer edge of the puckered hole, taking his first taste as he felt the impatient shifting of the angel's body.

"Yes...please...Talah..." Aridas drew his legs up, gripping them behind his knees. "Need this...need you..."

Talah pushed his tongue inside Aridas, enjoying the intimate taste of his lover. The sheer thought of being inside the angel was more than enough to make him painfully hard. The light dance of his fingers played over Aridas' balls and cock as he fucked him with his tongue.

"Talah...in me. Now."

Rising to his knees, Talah quickly wet his cock then leaned forward, running the head of his cock over the crack of Aridas' ass before entering the tight heat. Watching Aridas' face with a sharp intensity, Talah felt the resistance slowly give way to him. A low groan escaped him, and his hand moved to the angel's chest, pinching sharply at a hard nipple.

Aridas hissed, his back arching, driving his hips down, chest pushing up for more. "Yes..." Red eyes focused sharply on Talah. "Take me."

Once fully inside him, Talah rocked back and forth against Aridas. One hand slid down to the angel's hip, talons digging into his skin, keeping Aridas pinned in position. Hard thrusts repeatedly buried Talah's cock in Aridas, sharply increasing the pleasure.

Gasping, eyes widening, Aridas gripped Talah's arms. "Talah."

Talah couldn't look away from Aridas. He knew the body under him belonged to him. Every part of the angel was his. The thought escalated the sensations between them. "All mine. You're all mine."

His canines lengthened, and Talah bit Aridas' neck, lapping at the blood before his mouth fastened to the wounds. His hand slid between them, quickly stroking over Aridas' cock as he took him over and over again until everything exploded within him.

Aridas' back bowed and heat flooded them both, the fire blazing out of control, enveloping them in rich red-orange flames. "Mine."

The blaze rushed through Talah, sealing their bond, not only joined in body, but in mind, heart and soul as well. Talah froze as he nearly drowned in the all-consuming flames that forged their connection.

As the flames died down, flickering out of their own accord, Aridas held Talah to him. "All yours," he whispered.

Never having experienced anything like that in his life, Talah lay unmoving on top of Aridas, not in a real hurry to bring himself back to normal. He could feel the union of their hearts and minds. "As I am, Aridas."

"Always."

THE TRUE FALL OF

LUCIFER

Chapter One

Waving his hand in an indolent gesture, Lucifer dismissed the most annoying of the lower echelon. His patience level, never at its best, remained notoriously short lately. His lack of success in his latest endeavor had his minions paying the price.

His throne room, unlike what one would expect, was not fire and brimstone, but rivaled most in its claim to luxurious comfort. A black marble floor inlaid with silver patterning mirrored the occupants of the room in its depth. On its black stone throne Lucifer sprawled, clad in a loose, white silk shirt and black leather pants. Waves of rich, sable hair, dark as night, framed an angelically innocent face, yet his looks fooled none who truly knew him.

"The next one who annoys me with a report of failure will have to be cleaned up by the imps. Am I understood?" The mild tone did little to hide the temper underneath.

One of the bolder and possibly more foolish of Lucifer's minions stepped up to kneel before the dais. Cloaked in a coal black robe, the fallen angel bowed his head before speaking. "My Lord. I have just received a report regarding one of our own: Nias. It seems he has fallen in with one of Michael's angels."

Leveling a look at the one who dared to approach him, Lucifer stared for a long moment, yet nothing was visible in the darkness of his eyes. "Now why am I not surprised? Foolish Nias. However, your luck holds, Eton. I'm not in the mood to destroy you for that appalling piece of news. It just means I have to deal with it all myself, now doesn't it?"

Not expecting an answer, Lucifer rose slowly from his throne. Eton nodded and stood, backing away from the dais. No one with a sense of self-preservation turned a back to the Prince of Hell. Eton dissolved into the shadows without a word.

A dark cloak appeared, covering most of his form as Lucifer walked down the steps. Nobody dared to approach him, and quite a few took several steps backward. Temporarily trumped in his aim to balance the power of the cosmos, Lucifer wasn't about to let it stand in his way.

Before any eye could take in the lack of his presence, he was gone. He stepped out into the shielding form of night and the surrounding scenery gave him pause. It had been some time since he'd bothered to return to the first world of the universe. And in the interim, it had indeed changed. Contrary to popular belief, he had no use for its inhabitants, and hadn't since the Fall. After mortals turned their backs on the Fallen and what they had fought for, his embittered sense of betrayal refused to even dwell on the existence of humans.

"Oh. I've never seen you around here," a voice said from behind Lucifer. Its owner stepped away from the brick wall of a nearby building, clutching a lighter in his hand as he lit a cigarette. Taking a slow drag from it, he looked Lucifer up and down, his gaze hungry.

Lucifer stared at the being. To know the creatures he had once loved no longer even believed in him was a bitter pill to swallow. And he wanted to know none of them face to face. Only the chance at tapping into the essence of Michael's power had stirred Lucifer from his own realm. "And I'm someone you don't want to see either."

As Lucifer stepped closer to the young mortal, he raised his hand to the boy's chin. A gentle grip tilted his face as Lucifer studied him. Beneath the layers of chaos, Lucifer could still see the beauty of the creation. "You enjoy what you do, but you would rather be free to choose who you do it with. Instead, you are bound by your need to feed yourself and for a place to live. Is this the cause for the sadness you hide? You are Michael's creation."

The young man's mouth dropped open. Blinking, he just stared at Lucifer. "I love getting fucked, love sucking, but yeah, if it were up to me, I'd choose the guys. How the fuck did you know that? And who the fuck is Michael? My pop's name is Richard."

What Lucifer saw tugged at him. There was too much sadness stifling the beautiful light within. It seemed as if mortals did retain the same power over his kind, much to his regret. Sighing quietly, he lowered his hand. "Your human father doesn't interest me, child." Taking hold of the boy's hand, he pressed a card into it. "If you are wise,

187

you will seek out this address in the morning."

"Uh. Yeah." The hooker looked down at the card then back up at Lucifer. "My name's Raven—well, Trent, but everyone calls me Raven."

"Raven, there is too much of value inside you. Your life starts with that card. Use it wisely." Turning away, Lucifer made his way down the street. He wasn't far from his intended target.

CA

From his perch atop a three-story building, Michael watched the scene play out below. As Lucifer walked away from the young man, Michael just shook his head. Lifting a hand, he erased any memory of what had transpired and destroyed the card. He was not one to interfere in the lives of men in such direct ways, but at times it was necessary. Jumping down to the alley between two buildings, Michael waited.

Lucifer proceeded to turn down the alley as a short cut to the next street. Then he stilled abruptly, the tension of his body revealing his awareness of Michael. His creator was not too far off. He stubbornly resisted the assailing sense even as it rippled through him. Narrowing his eyes, he rapidly rethought his plans. Lucifer had no desire to come across Michael at this point. As he backed up, he had every intention of returning to his own realm.

"And where might you be going?"

Emerging from the shadows, Michael walked toward

Lucifer. Emerald wings as long as he was tall at nearly six and a half feet twitched as a breeze blew through the alley. Blond hair spilled over his shoulders, and he stopped just in front of Lucifer, arms crossed.

"This is not your realm."

"That would be my business, not yours, Michael."

"You've grown more impertinent," Michael said coolly. "And you are gravely mistaken." The Archangel's blue gaze sharpened as he stared at Lucifer. "Everything here is my business," Michael whispered, his voice stern and deep.

Once the most beloved and trusted of Michael's creations, Lucifer now felt the coldness of separation more keenly with his creator's closer proximity. Yet he hid the depth of it within himself. "They no longer even believe in me. And the few who do..." He trailed off, unable to even complete the sentence. "What I want has nothing to do with your creation." Not about to get into a war of words with Michael, Lucifer abruptly disappeared to return to his own throne room.

"You cannot run from me. I am a part of you, just as you are a part of me."

Lucifer shut out the words echoing in his mind as several of his minions scattered with his sudden reappearance. He hadn't expected to come face-to-face with Michael. Stalking from the room, he headed into the corridor toward his own private quarters.

"You were my finest creation."

As he shut the door, Lucifer heard the voice and whirled around. The massive gilt mirror on his wall reflected the image of his creator back at him.

"No longer. I am nothing to you." Lucifer turned his back on the image, ignoring Michael.

"There was a time...when you were everything to me," Michael said.

Closing his eyes, Lucifer tried desperately to shut out the voice. The cloak dissolved into his wings. The ebony shield protected him as Lucifer lay on the bed. "That time is no more, Michael."

"Yet a part of you still longs for it."

"You delude yourself." Lucifer's voice lacked the conviction to give truth to the words. Opening his eyes, he stared at his own reflection in one of the other mirrors.

"Do I?" The mirror's surface shimmered like water on a pond, and an incorporeal figure stepped out into the room. Michael's form was nearly translucent as he stared down at Lucifer.

Lucifer abruptly sat up, giving Michael a challenging look. "I don't need you. I never have. Your great age has confused your memory."

"Your eyes betray your words." Michael's voice seemed to vibrate around them, blanketing the air. "Fallen or no, you are still mine."

Lucifer sneered. "You are mistaken. I belong to none but myself. I was shut out, forgotten and left here. I need nothing and want nothing from you."

"Your arrogance and pride landed you here," Michael countered. The silver material of his short tunic sparkled in the light from the torches scattered about the room as Michael moved closer to the bed. "You forget that it was I who made you, I who gave you life, who taught you to love and be loved."

Lucifer stood, facing the transparent form, his wings twitching restlessly. He could feel Michael's presence seeping into his entire being. "And you are forgetting to leave me alone to wallow in the misery."

"We are two halves of the same being," Michael said. "Two halves of one soul."

"I am my own, Michael."

Michael reached out, ghost-like fingers touching Lucifer's. "Denial does not change fact."

For a moment, Lucifer tried to hold onto Michael's hand, longing for what once was burned within him. Jerking back, he fisted his hands at his side. "This is my world now. The illusion that hides the despair and misery of others."

If there was pain within Michael, he did not show it. Letting his arm fall back to his side, he simply nodded. "You can deny me all you like, but it will not change the truth: I am within you." With that, his image faded away.

Lucifer tried to reach for him, to grasp whatever he could of what was left. His pride had always gotten in the way and left him with nothing. Searing pain rocked through him, everything he had locked away brought out in a moment. "Michael, please," he whispered to the empty air. The second he acknowledged it, Lucifer tried desperately to shove it back down as he returned to his bed.

Ruthlessly, he dealt with the very thing that tried to rise in him. Only when the void returned to his soul did he finally relax. A lazy wave of his hand opened his chamber doors. His minions entered, the sound of their laughter filling the room.

Some of them draped themselves across his bed, and the others lounged on the scattered pillows on the floor. As he closed his eyes, hands reached for him, smoothing over his flesh in feather-light caresses. Some of the Fallen maintained a male form and some chose female. The union of angels was a far different thing, something Lucifer had known only with Michael. The physical mating of humans was all that was left to him, and its pleasures were sufficient. Or so he told himself.

Complacent for but a moment beneath the fondling, Lucifer stretched beneath the hands before he reached for one of the males. With a forceful pressure, he flipped Ananan over onto his stomach. Rising to his hands and knees, the other demon stared over his shoulder at Lucifer with lust-filled eyes. With no warning or preparation, Lucifer's talons pierced Ananan's hip, and a hard grip pulled him back, impaling Ananan on the dark angel's cock. A cry filled with pleasure and pain reached Lucifer as he relentlessly took what he wanted.

The tight pressure of his hands rocked Ananan's hips, pulling his ass back into every brutal thrust. Lucifer could only briefly lose himself in the union. Even as the inexorable pressure built up in him, a pained cry escaped Lucifer, reaching into the Heavens themselves. His soul was truly lost and had no place to go. The haunting lamentation had no words; its music was a fragile sound drifting in the space between time and reality. The song was heard but not answered.

Chapter Two

It had taken Lucifer a bit of time to trace the elusive mage. The conflicting reports he'd heard hadn't helped matters any. Finally, Lucifer received a reliable message about where the mage had been hiding. The wizard had indeed done the unthinkable—he'd tapped into the very essence of the power of the cosmos. It should have been a relatively easy thing for Lucifer to gain for himself, yet thus far it hadn't proven easy at all.

Leaving his minions behind, Lucifer reluctantly returned to Earth. It would have been better if the mage maintained his own realm instead of Lucifer having to traipse around a place he hated to be in. Yet he couldn't give up the chance to gain the power for himself. He needed it for more reasons than he allowed himself to dwell on.

The house was dark with no discernible lights on anywhere inside. The neighborhood was generally quiet, the streets empty, leaving only the occasional shadow of a cat running across the street.

"For someone who despises this place, you seem to return to it time and again."

"Maybe I'm just getting to know the place once more." Lucifer faced Michael with a casual shrug. "It needn't concern you."

Pushing away from the tree he'd been leaning against, Michael walked over to him, standing close enough to touch, though he didn't. "And since when have you taken to craving the company of mortals?" There was more to be said, but it went unspoken. Michael's eyes made the rest crystal clear.

"Isn't it about time I crawled out of my hole?"

"Or is it that you want it filled again?" Michael took to the air, touching down with grace on the rooftop of the house they'd both been watching.

Moonlight filtered through the clouds above and gave Lucifer's wings a glistening, ghostly appearance as they stretched to their full span. He landed near Michael. "Oh, that's been filled many a time, Michael."

Michael lifted an eyebrow. "Somehow," he whispered, moving closer, "I doubt that."

Turning his back on Michael, Lucifer stared out at the neighborhood. "I hate to disappoint you on that. So if it makes you feel better, I'll lie and say it hasn't been."

Michael slid a fingertip over the top of Lucifer's left wing as he whispered in his ear, "You cannot lie to me. Your soul and body remember, even if your mind has chosen to forget."

Lucifer growled softly. No part of him had ever forgotten what it had been like to be with Michael. He had

195

craved it for eons. Fighting the desire to lean back, Lucifer simply shook his head. "Do you believe it was ever easy to forget, Michael?"

Sliding his fingers through Lucifer's hair, Michael pulled back his head, lips ghosting over Lucifer's ear. "Do you think it has been easy for me? Do you think I don't crave your touch still?"

"I think it was easy for you, yes." After so many ages passed, Lucifer no longer was assured of anything concerning Michael. Closing his eyes, he turned his head slightly, unable to stop himself from pressing closer to the touch of those lips, not even when his rational mind demanded he move away before he became entrapped. "I no longer know you."

"Two halves," Michael breathed across Lucifer's lips. "I still need you."

"And I told you, I need nothing." Closing the distance, Lucifer captured Michael's mouth with his own, if only to prove to himself there was no longer anything there. Michael turned Lucifer until they were facing then folded his wings around them. Fingers sliding through Lucifer's hair, Michael pushed his tongue deep into Lucifer's mouth, swept through it, touching on memories best left untapped. The warmth of Michael's presence flooded Lucifer's soul. For a moment, Lucifer allowed himself to feel the hunger he'd so carefully hidden. An edge of desperation crept into his actions before he could stop it. His fingers tangled within his creator's hair, remembering the silkiness, the sensations of it drifting over his skin.

Using nothing more than a single thread of thought, Michael took them away from there, into the place between the realms of Heaven, Earth and Hell. The room, if it could be called that, was cut into a towering mountain. Michael backed Lucifer against the smooth stone, hunger growing as the kiss deepened. His knee lodged between Lucifer's thighs, tight against his body. He slid his fingers down the edges of Lucifer's wings, knowing where the most sensitive spots were, where a single touch could spark an inferno.

Lucifer couldn't escape now and knew it. Michael held him captive and in the palm of his hand. He parted his legs and couldn't stop himself from rubbing against Michael's thigh as a shudder rolled through him. The small spark became a rage of need, to feel everything he could—even if just one more time.

"Yes," Michael whispered as he worked the leather pants open. He pressed harder against Lucifer, giving him some friction. Once Lucifer's pants were undone, Michael pushed them down his hips. "Ride me."

Lucifer lost himself in the feel of the fingers around him. His hips jerked as he began to fuck Michael's hand. Closing his eyes, Lucifer tipped his head back against the wall as he obeyed the need and instinct of his body. Edging his hand between them, he pressed his palm against the front of Michael's pants, adding his own friction to the mix. The familiar, delicious sensations drenched him. Right or wrong, it didn't matter at this moment in time.

Michael recaptured Lucifer's mouth, tongue sliding

deep as he spread Lucifer's legs apart. With a shift of his hips, Michael had Lucifer's legs around him, his cock freed with a simple tug to the tie on his pants. All it took was a swift thrust to drive him deep inside Lucifer's body.

The swift penetration brought with it burning pain, along with searing pleasure. Lucifer had never known another like this, had never wanted to. This part of him belonged truly to his creator. Using his hands on Michael's shoulders for leverage, he pushed down harder, impaling himself fully on Michael.

Pinning him against the wall, Michael thrust hard and fast, driving deep inside, over and over. Every inch of his body, every shred of his soul, needed this, need to feel the heat and rage and need that only Lucifer could give him.

"Part of me," he said, the words followed by a low growl into Lucifer's mouth. Michael doubled his efforts, fist stroking over Lucifer's cock, thumb probing the slit on every upstroke.

A chaotic swirl of emotions answered Michael. Lucifer no longer knew where he began or ended. Connected to his creator, Lucifer could only swim in the swift current of sensations that overrode all sense and reason. Insatiable, devouring need washed over him. Then it all exploded and he shuddered. Every muscle tightened in the near painful, exhilarating release. "Michael!"

"Mine." The word was partly said, partly growled, Michael thrusting several more times before lightning raced up his spine and out his cock, filling Lucifer with near-blinding brilliance.

Lucifer became blind to everything but what filled him. The light burned him and took him over, leaving him to fall into the overwhelming expanse of infinity itself. Surrounded only by Michael's essence, Lucifer momentarily lost himself in the exquisite bliss.

Slowly coming down, Lucifer refused to acknowledge the one word as he collapsed against Michael. Resting his forehead to the angel's shoulder, Lucifer resisted the very implication. Though his soul longed for the eternal completion of himself, a barrier of ice and pain kept him from expressing it.

"I am always with you," Michael whispered into Lucifer's ear. "I am a part of you."

෪

It had taken only the short time in his creator's presence to leave Lucifer battling the memories fighting to be free. A familiar coldness descended over him, and he held to it like a shield. Yet it was no longer enough. With baleful eyes, he watched his minions as he sprawled on his throne. The angelic beauty of his face and form remained unmarred, and he appeared hauntingly distant to those around him. The illusion served him well.

Once he had been the first angel of the Order of Creation, the Heart of Michael. Now he was nothing. He had been the highest of the Three: Adonai, the Hand of Michael, and Gabriel, the voice of Michael. They had governed the universe in its order until men and women were created.

After the Fall, humanity itself had become a bane to Lucifer's existence. It blamed him for its misery. Easier to believe demons were at fault for a man raping his child or a woman killing her spouse. Far easier than to face the truth. Some demons did exist solely to exact revenge on the creation they had once loved and fought for, but not all evil was perpetrated by them. In his brethrens' souls, it had all become twisted into a perversion of its former self. Still, mankind bore the brunt of its own inhumanity, but they simply refused to accept it. Those who didn't blame it on Lucifer, blamed it on God.

Outside of Lucifer's domain, others of the Fallen wallowed in their own torment. They had created the barren landscape of their own pain and hatred, most of the hatred directed at themselves in punishment for their disobedience to Michael. Lucifer had refused to bow down. At the time, their battle had been just. In the intervening age, Lucifer finally realized Michael had been right. Their kind hadn't been meant to guide humanity as they'd wanted. It was a bitter pill for him to swallow. Everything they had stood for had been rejected completely by the creatures the angels had loved so dearly. Even to the point of turning the Morning Star into evil incarnate, and giving Lucifer and the Fallen the blame for the ills of the world. If they had been among the mortals when this lesson became apparent, it would have completely destroyed them all.

How could it have all gone so wrong? The shining light that had once been his soul dimmed. Lucifer had locked himself away from the mortal plane, but it still haunted him. Even when mortals found themselves in his realm, he ignored them for the most part. Not so oddly, many remained outside, punishing themselves for their perceived disobedience to God, just as some of his brethren did. A few reached his gates, and he allowed them in. He interfered with none. Lucifer simply refused to deal with them.

Closing his eyes, he remembered the indescribable feeling of being in Michael's presence. It had been that way for most of his existence. There were no words, only a steady stream of the peaceful bliss enshrouding him. Michael had been his existence, the sole reason for his being. When that had been torn from him, Lucifer had raged for time unknown. He'd laid complete waste to the realm in which he'd been imprisoned. After emerging from the ashes, he had created this place, and hidden himself away. The wounds on his soul were still raw, as if it had all just happened, but there was no longer any anger— only emptiness.

The battle itself had lost meaning. Humanity was nothing to him. Nothing more than Michael's creation as it should have always been. Whatever Lucifer had felt had been taken by humanity itself. Better that they had forgotten him. Lucifer still felt betrayed by them, but now he understood his own culpability.

In all of this time, he had forged his own kind of existence. He felt it being threatened again, simply by being in Michael's presence. Anger once again rose in him. He did not need Michael.

He hadn't wanted to hear those words Michael had said to him. Yet they played relentlessly in his mind even after he'd high-tailed it back to his own realm. His power had closed off his empire from any outside influence, refusing to allow in even a whisper of what had happened. Should his minions become aware of what had transpired, they would turn on him. He couldn't afford the chaos, not with his own grasp on himself so tenuous.

Once again he found himself haunted by the mesmerizing vision of Michael's eyes, and the indelible memories of the Archangel's touch. Lucifer had done his best to freeze it all out of his soul over the eons, only to find he hadn't succeeded at all. His heart and soul needed to call out, but he refused to allow it voice.

He stalked down the steps of the dais and restlessly paced in front of it. Every outlet he had tried left him more agitated. Nothing sated him, and he found no release from his own internal suffering.

His body stiffened as he felt the invisible wave pulsing through his entire realm. Its resonance awakened something inside him. Quickly he looked around for Michael, at first thinking his creator had come to him. A second later he realized the truth.

"That damn mage." Lucifer knew the signature of the overwhelming power as it surged through the cosmos. The aftereffect rippled in waves of lesser intensity. It was the essence of Michael, yet not Michael. Lucifer wanted and needed that for himself. If he could have it and not have to deal with Michael, so much the better.

His wings folded into his back and the illusion of a black cloak took their place. A breath later, he was in the mage's house. So much easier to get directly to the source now. A low thrum, unheard by mortal ears, vibrated through the walls and floors of the house. It echoed within Lucifer, freezing him for a split second. The very core of creation whispered within the streams of power. It started as a tingle, running straight through Lucifer's soul.

The room glowed with an unearthly light, beyond the spectrum of mortal sight. It bathed the two occupants of the room, seen only by Lucifer's eyes. A hypnotic swirl of energy beckoned to the demon as it twined around him, recognizing a weaker source of itself. Lucifer was unaware of his movement toward the center of that power. Even as his outer shell began to burn, he didn't feel it.

An explosion of thunder rattled the house, shaking the walls from the foundation to the roof. As the winds stirred outside, the sound resembled that of a freight train barreling down on the house itself. The cone of power flickered and pulsed, threatening to consume everything it could.

Chapter Three

Michael sat on his throne, deep in thought. While his body might be where it should've been, his mind was not. He'd gotten through the barriers once more, but it was nothing but a single hole in a wall of ice thicker than the first world itself. He was not without hope, however. He knew he'd started the chain reaction within Lucifer, knew Lucifer could still feel him. They were connected, just as he'd told Lucifer: two halves of one soul.

As he sat there thinking, Michael became aware of something...not quite right. As the energy grew, he closed his eyes, tracing its path to the source. What he saw then set his heart racing. Without a second to spare, he spirited down to Earth, into the house of a man who should have never learned the arts he knew.

Outside of the sphere of Michael's control, the energy could obliterate Lucifer. Oblivious to his own danger, the dark angel walked in a daze toward the very thing he so desperately needed. Unable to distinguish between the power and his creator, Lucifer succumbed to the energy as it beckoned him. A sudden flare of brilliance blinded him, burning into his eyes, yet still he moved forward. It was everything he was, stripped bared. As illusion slipped away from Lucifer, his wings unfurled.

The sudden vision of Lucifer in the room in all of his angelic beauty left the room's inhabitants frozen in fear and awe. A stronger surge of the very same power that drew him rolled through the room as Michael appeared. Stilling, Lucifer turned sightless eyes toward his creator. Outside, thunder chased the wind as both increased in intensity.

Lifting a hand, Michael beckoned to him. "Come." His voice echoed in the room, the thunder and wind making it sound larger than life.

The mortal occupants seemed frozen, their eyes unblinking, and their faces fixed in disbelief. Michael reached out, taking one of Lucifer's hands, letting Lucifer feel the twin rhythms of their powers together.

"It cannot give you what you seek. Only I can."

"Michael," Lucifer called to his creator. He could feel Michael, yet could not see him. Darkness had swallowed his vision, and he had been left completely defenseless. The weaker sense of the original power no longer called to him, but its energy ate at his skin like acid.

Enveloping them both in his wings, Michael freed the mortals from their frozen state just as he vanished, Lucifer held tight in his arms.

Back in the cave between the realms, he placed Lucifer on the stone floor, smoothing the raven hair from Lucifer's forehead.

"What have you done?" he whispered.

Pain was there, and it settled deep into Lucifer. His eyes had been burned and his skin and wings ravaged by the exposure. The soft touch of Michael's hand eased far more than the physical damage. "I thought I could have you."

"But you do have me." Michael kissed Lucifer's forehead, the warmth and light seeping into Lucifer's body to heal the damage the mage's toying had done. "You have always had me," he repeated, lips sliding over Lucifer's face, down to his mouth. "Always."

"Without the aggravation." Only then did Lucifer finally realize his actions could have destroyed him completely. The blackness clouding his vision started to clear as the healing light flowed over him, and the wounds left on his body began to heal and fade. When he could clearly see Michael, he reached up to his creator's hair, fingers smoothing over its golden length.

"If I wasn't here to aggravate you," Michael murmured against his lips, "then what purpose would you have to exist?"

"I would have no purpose at all. And I thought I was the one who was supposed to aggravate you." Drawing strands of Michael's hair toward him, Lucifer let it fall over his own chest. The contrast between the darkness of his own hair and Michael's were like night and day.

"Oh, believe me, you are most aggravating." Michael closed the scant distance between them, lips closing over Lucifer's.

"Yet still you want me." Ever one to have to have the

last word, Lucifer opened to Michael's kiss.

"Always." Chuckling into the kiss, Michael set out to drive Lucifer so insane with need that thought was no longer possible.

Lucifer caught the idea from Michael and decided to resist the attempt for as long as he could. Or at the very least turn the tables on the angel. He slid his fingers beneath the wave of Michael's hair, caressing the side of his throat. Slow, leisurely strokes of Lucifer's tongue played against Michael's as if they had all of eternity. A soft moan slipped into the kiss, and Michael settled over Lucifer, bracing himself on his forearms as he deepened the kiss, rocking his hips over Lucifer's.

Too much clothing got in the way of Lucifer's explorations. As one hand played at Michael's throat, Lucifer slipped the other beneath the edge of the angel's tunic. A slow drift of his fingers traveled over the bare skin, relearning the feel of his lover. Lucifer wanted to touch as much as he wanted to be touched. He wrapped his legs around Michael's waist and arched. Drawing back from the kiss, he whispered, "We have time, Michael. Let me love you again."

Michael sat up, pulling his tunic off as he did. Then he started on his pants, pulling the tie loose, his gaze never leaving Lucifer's. Lucifer watched him intently. "I am your other half," Michael said quietly, arms and wings outstretched.

"Eternally mine." A thread of satisfaction wove through the words. In the space between their worlds,

Lucifer felt free of the concerns that could take his attention away from Michael. Standing slowly, he undressed as well. As much as he wanted to touch the magnificent spread of wings, he knew things would spiral too quickly out of their control if he did. "Remind me to teach you a bit about luxury," he murmured as he willed a large bed, draped in red silk, to appear. Moving in on Michael, Lucifer flattened his palms on Michael's chest, caressing over the smooth muscles as he gently pushed the Archangel toward the bed.

Michael chuckled softly. "Ever the prideful one." As soon as he touched the bed, he fell back onto it, reaching out for Lucifer. "Show me you believe. Show me that I am yours."

Part of Lucifer's problem had always been that at times he couldn't believe in what they'd had. He'd lost sight in his own internal struggles. Lucifer hovered over Michael and trailed his fingers over every inch of skin bared to him in soft caresses. As he set his teeth around Michael's right nipple, his hand traveled over the taut muscles of his lover's stomach.

Michael hissed, pushing his chest up for more. "Yes."

Too much time had gone by since Lucifer had wiled away the nights in his creator's arms. Biting gently, he tugged at Michael's flesh. Lucifer made love to Michael with his mouth and hands, content for the time being. His body could wait for a short time while he sated his need for the taste of Michael. Releasing Michael's nipple, Lucifer scattered kisses over Michael's stomach, working his way downward. The tip of his tongue circled slowly over Michael's navel as his fingers caressed the Archangel's inner thigh.

Parting his legs, Michael closed his eyes, losing himself in this, in this touch he craved more than anything in existence. Just as he was a part of Lucifer, Lucifer was a part of him. He could feel Lucifer in his soul just as well as he could feel the Fallen angel's touch on his skin. "Eternally yours."

A soft growl answered Michael right before Lucifer's head lowered farther. Nestled between his legs, Lucifer caressed Michael's thighs as he raised his gaze to Michael's face. Then Lucifer swallowed Michael's cock.

"My soul." A quiet whisper of Lucifer's thoughts reached Michael, the only thing intruding on the exquisite heat.

"Yes!" Michael's eyes flew open and he looked down. "Please. My love, my soul." Groaning, he spread his legs farther, wanting everything, wanting Lucifer everywhere.

As Michael opened to him, Lucifer caressed the curve of his lover's ass before ghosting along the crease. A slow burning sensation lingered over Michael's skin, increasing with each touch from Lucifer, and flickers of pleasure followed in their wake. Lucifer engulfed the hard length of the Archangel's cock before pulling back, a quick flick of his tongue opening the small slit. He drank in the spoken words and the message beneath him. Michael needed to belong to him as much as Lucifer needed the same. In answer, part of what held him back began to thaw and his own emotions seeped through, blanketing the angel.

Michael's breath left him, every touch, every slide of Lucifer's fingers and tongue, sending him soaring higher than any wings could ever take him. He wanted to touch, to kiss, to taste; wanted to feel Lucifer around him, within him.

"Please. I need you. Inside me. Filling me."

Lifting his head, Lucifer said softly, "After I've had my full taste of you, Michael." The angel's pleading, breathless voice affected him, and Lucifer damn near lost it. He dipped his head back down. The slide of his tongue probed over the crease of Michael's ass and his hands spread him open. Lucifer's tongue lengthened as it entered the depths of Michael's body.

Michael cried out, trembling in Lucifer's hands. He rocked his hips, driving Lucifer's tongue deeper. Lucifer answered the need, felt it in every inch of his being as Michael cried out. Warmth ignited from Lucifer as his tongue plunged repeatedly into Michael's writhing body. It spread quickly through the angel, and when his tongue withdrew, Lucifer surged up, thrusting into Michael.

Gripping Lucifer's shoulders and wrapping his legs around Lucifer's waist, Michael thrust his hips upward, gasping as the dark angel drove deeper inside him. "Take me. Show me I'm yours," he growled out, body writhing beneath Lucifer.

Each word spoken by the angel was greeted by a forceful thrust of Lucifer's hips. Lucifer held Michael captive, hands on the Archangel's hips, tugging Michael into every brutal thrust. Talons dug into Michael's skin, but didn't break the surface.

Grabbing Lucifer's head, Michael pulled him down, growling into Lucifer's mouth, "Take. Me."

For a moment, he resisted what Michael demanded of him. Lucifer knew what it meant. If he allowed it, any separation between them would tear him completely asunder. He wanted the carnal beast to swallow him whole and allow him no thought. His talons pierced Michael's skin, blood seeping from the wounds as the sharp nails dug deeply into him. Throwing back his head, Lucifer cried out sharply as his soul struggled for balance.

Unable to stop the demand for their true union, everything within him poured into the angel. It sought its creator, the other half of his soul, his twin. They were the light and the dark. Neither could exist without the other. Lucifer began to tremble, and everything within him relentlessly commanded Michael to give the same. Lucifer's soul took without asking and his orgasm sent him spiraling out of control.

Brilliance filled them both, Michael chanting Lucifer's name as their souls wound tight, fusing together until it was impossible to know where one ended and the other began. Michael's nails left sharp stinging trails down Lucifer's back, the flames bursting forth and surrounding them both as Michael jerked, coming in a rush that left them both dazed and breathless. Tears streamed down his face as he clung to Lucifer, shaking uncontrollably.

They were one soul in two forms, one and the same. Lucifer's cry joined Michael's as memories he'd long forced himself to forget, surfaced. Michael had given up half his soul in the creation of Lucifer. His head bowed to Michael's shoulder, wetting his lover's skin with his own tears.

Michael murmured words of love and comfort, soothing strokes sliding over Lucifer. His heart raced, its twin echo beating from the being above him. He could feel Lucifer within him—a rich, soul-deep sensation that left him awestruck. "You are sacred to me," he whispered.

"Forgive me. I had forgotten." The pain in Lucifer's voice was clear. "You made me; I am you." Lucifer's face burrowed against Michael's throat. His talons released their hold and his hands caressed over the wounds, healing them in a loving touch.

"There is nothing to forgive." Michael lifted Lucifer's head, needing to see his face, his eyes. "We are one."

About the Author

To learn more about Mychael Black and Shayne Carmichael, please visit www.theprincesangel.com and www.mychaelblack.com. Send an email to Mychael at mychael_black@yahoo.com or to Shayne at shayne@theprincesangel.com or join their Yahoo! group to join in the fun with other readers as well as Mychael and Shayne!

http://groups.yahoo.com/group/theprincesangel/

Enter into a world of magic, lust, love and betrayal.

Magic and the Pagan
© 2007 Mychael Black and
Shayne Carmichael

Evan Bartholomew lives life as a gay pagan with a deep interest in magic. Not wise choices in the small town where he resides. When he comes across a book of magic in an old bookstore, he fantasizes about the portrait of a man within its pages.

The first time Evan attempts one of the spells in the book, he finds himself in a world he never knew existed, completely clueless. A world of demons, magic, a queen who wants to kill him, a king who lusts after him, and the man of his fantasies, Aidan Loriel.

Available now in ebook and print from Samhain Publishing.

A world away and centuries past, nothing in this feudal kingdom is ordinary—especially love.

On Wings of Blue
© 2008 Anne Cain

Eiji is a young traveling musician whose skill with the *shamisen* attracts almost as many would-be consorts as his handsome features do. But his beauty also draws the attention of a ruthless warlord who won't be denied. Unless Eiji gives himself in every way to this man, his life will be forfeit...before he's even known what it is to experience true love.

Then a small act of kindness to a helpless butterfly changes the course of his destiny.

A creature of magic, Hakusa begs the gods for a chance to be joined with Eiji forever, even if it means giving up everything he has ever known. But his choice to become human comes with a cruel price.

Hakusa vows to rescue Eiji from the warlord's scheme. But like delicate notes of the *shamisen,* his unearthly magic is slowly fading away.

Just when he needs it most.

Available now in ebook from Samhain Publishing.

GREAT CHEAP FUN

Discover eBooks!

THE FASTEST WAY TO GET THE HOTTEST NAMES

Get your favorite authors on your favorite reader, long before they're out in print! Ebooks from Samhain go wherever you go, and work with whatever you carry—Palm, PDF, Mobi, and more.

 Samhain Publishing ltd

Printed in the United Kingdom by
Lightning Source UK Ltd., Milton Keynes
137429UK00001B/82/P